P9-BZA-564

RAW DEAL

A novelization by
Walter Wager

Based on the screenplay by **Gary M. DeVore**
and **Norman Wexler**

WARNER BOOKS

A Warner Communications Company

WARNER BOOKS EDITION

Copyright © 1986 by Famous Films, B. V.
All rights reserved.

Warner Books, Inc.
666 Fifth Avenue
New York, N.Y. 10103

 A Warner Communications Company

Printed in the United States of America

First Printing: June, 1986

10 9 8 7 6 5 4 3 2 1

5/08 ℓ

Kaminski saw the huge vehicle moving towards him.

The truck was a monster no bullets could stop. Kaminski twisted the wheel of his Cadillac violently to spin it off in the opposite direction.

Another mechanical giant was grinding towards him. It was a massive Caterpillar Loader. There was no place to dodge. Bullets were raking the Cadillac from three directions. The two enormous vehicles were closing in steadily.

30 yards.

20.

10.

Kaminski jerked open the door beside him and rolled out seconds before the Cadillac was crushed between the monsters. The drivers of those machines were shouting in triumph, unaware that he wasn't being pulped inside.

They found out when he raised his shotgun and blew away one third of the Caterpillar jockey's head. . .

RAW DEAL

ATTENTION: SCHOOLS AND CORPORATIONS

WARNER books are available at quantity discounts with bulk purchase for educational, business, or sales promotional use. For information, please write to: SPECIAL SALES DEPARTMENT, WARNER BOOKS, 666 FIFTH AVENUE, NEW YORK, N.Y. 10103.

**ARE THERE WARNER BOOKS
YOU WANT BUT CANNOT FIND IN YOUR LOCAL STORES?**

You can get any WARNER BOOKS title in print. Simply send title and retail price, plus 50¢ per order and 50¢ per copy to cover mailing and handling costs for each book desired. New York State and California residents add applicable sales tax. Enclose check or money order only, no cash please, to: WARNER BOOKS, P.O. BOX 690, NEW YORK, N.Y. 10019.

1

There are autumn days that make you glad to be alive. This wasn't one of them.

No golden Indian summer sun blessed northeastern Illinois this dull October morning.

It wasn't clear, crisp football weather, either.

Rain had fallen off and on since dawn, and the concrete runways of the small country airport glistened with a hundred puddles. The sullen sky above was an almost solid roof of slate-gray clouds. Walled with dark cinder blocks, the one-story operations building was equally drab. The soaked wind sock atop the pole nearby hung lifeless—a drowned corpse.

Suddenly there was a low, metallic growl overhead.

The noise grew louder.

It built swiftly to a roar as a small twin-engine plane punched through the clouds three hundred feet above the far end of the main runway. The lanky pilot of the chartered Beechcraft deftly eased the altitude control forward, guided his machine to a perfect landing and taxied the plane to within forty yards of the operations building.

He cut the engines and clicked loose his safety harness. Then he walked back to the main compartment and spoke to the lone passenger.

"We're here," the pilot said as he opened the door and released the steps.

The passenger didn't answer. He hadn't said a word from the moment he'd shown up to board the Beechcraft some ninety-five minutes earlier. He was an ordinary-looking man of medium build with a plain face and neatly trimmed brown hair. His standard blue suit marked him as a middle-level executive.

The veteran pilot had recognized that immediately.

He'd flown a lot of them.

It wasn't unusual for preoccupied business types not to talk to him. They were obsessive company men who thought only of the sale . . . the meeting . . . the deal.

This Arnold Flood was typical of that breed.

Just another earnest soldier in some corporate army.

The charter pilot was wrong.

The driver's license and other ID the passenger carried were all forged. His name wasn't Arnold Flood, and the powerful army in which he served was not incorporated. His silence did not reflect preoccupation. He didn't want the pilot to remember his voice.

Always offer strangers a minimum profile.

It was a basic survival rule.

The man in the blue suit descended to the runway and sniffed the damp air. He glanced neither left nor right. He wasn't the least bit interested in this place. He wasn't going to stay, and he'd probably never be back. He was here now only because some man he'd never met had ordered him to do so.

Now he saw the nondescript brown station wagon beside the operations building. A thin plume of exhaust signaled that the engine was running. He walked toward it briskly. There was a schedule to keep. It all had been planned by someone whose name he didn't even know.

The man who wasn't Arnold Flood got into the station wagon and buckled up his seat belt. It would be unprofessional to take any unnecessary chances. He didn't say anything to the driver, and the man behind the wheel didn't speak, either.

He merely grunted as he put the vehicle in gear. The station wagon began to move, and six minutes later it was cruising steadily down the highway—heading west.

the surface of the

There are small, nervous waves everywhere,
but none of them serious.

The boat, the Island, Maud Floor, i t him, the Heavy

He was very strong. Despite the weight, he swung the

2

Gusts of wind rumpled the surface of the huge lake.
There were small, nervous waves everywhere,
but none of them serious.

More than three hundred miles long and over one hundred
miles wide, Lake Michigan was too big to be bothered by
minor breezes.

The twenty-eight-foot cabin cruiser cut evenly through
the choppy waters, moving untroubled toward the shore half
a mile away. The fog had lifted an hour earlier, and the men
in the boat could see the small pier clearly.

There was no one on it or nearby.

That was good.

The cruiser moved up to the dock, maneuvered slowly,
and slid alongside. A bulky man in sunglasses and a
knee-length zippered jacket jumped onto the dock, moving
with surprising agility for someone his size. He carried a
three-foot-long canvas bag, the kind a professional athlete
might use. It was filled with the heavy tools of his unusual
trade.

He was very strong. Despite the weight, he swung the

bag with easy confidence. He watched patiently as the cruiser pulled away from the dock, standing motionless until it was only a small dot.

Now he took a deep breath, savoring the clean, moist air of this inland sea. Then he turned and looked up the shore—first one way and then the other. There was no one in sight. He nodded, glanced at his wristwatch, and saw that he was three minutes ahead of schedule.

He nodded again as he strode up the dock toward the asphalt-topped road.

In his trade it was very important to be on time.

Being late could be fatal.

3

It's obvious and not the least bit surprising.

A railroad station reflects the style and needs of the place it serves.

Union Station in downtown Chicago really represents the Windy City. It's big and busy and seething with energy, full of no-nonsense people who know exactly where they're going. Nobody dawdles in Union Station. It's a place for doers, not dreamers.

Like Chicago, Union Station is dynamic and works hard. Tens of thousands of purposeful people pour through it every day. Long-distance and commuter trains by the hundreds move these legions in and out around the clock. It's strictly routine. Nobody pays any attention to them.

Nobody noticed the commuter train from the suburbs that pulled in at ten minutes before noon. No one gave a second glance to the squinty-eyed man in the tan raincoat who disembarked from the third car. A dozen other passengers got off before he did, and a score more followed.

More than a hundred others poured from the train, and they all hurried down the platform into the terminal. He was just part of the human torrent. When they entered the main hall of the station, he barely slowed as he spotted the big clock.

For a moment his narrow, dark eyes glowed with something. It wasn't anything pleasant.

Neither was he.

Everyone who'd ever worked with him considered him a nasty son of a bitch.

One of them was watching him now. It was the driver of the station wagon that had waited at the small airport. He saw the man from the train scan the crowd warily, his squinty eyes gleaming like polished daggers.

Then he noticed the driver. No flicker of recognition showed on either of their faces. It was as if they looked right through each other. A moment later he followed the driver out of the terminal.

When they reached the station wagon, the front seat was empty. There were two men on the seat behind it. One was the passenger from the Beechcraft. The other was the traveler who had come ashore from the cabin cruiser. They made room for the man from the train to join them, and the driver slid in behind the wheel.

He guided the big Chrysler wagon carefully through the heavy downtown traffic. He didn't speak or turn on the radio. He was completely focused on driving. It was his job to get them there, and he wasn't about to make any mistakes. The people who were paying him did not tolerate mistakes.

As he patiently maneuvered the vehicle away from the center of the city, the men on the seat behind stared out the windows silently. There wasn't anything to say. They were skilled craftsmen on their way to a high-paying job. They knew their work and they knew each other. There was no reason for small talk.

Soon they were beyond the suburbs. Traffic was much lighter, but the driver never took his eyes from the road. His concentration was intense, total. Mile by mile, houses grew fewer and trees more numerous. Chicago was two hours behind them when the man from the boat reached into the cargo space behind him. He pulled out the large canvas bag he'd carried ashore.

He laid it across his knees and zipped it open.

There was a 30.06-caliber semiautomatic rifle. Taped to the barrel were a screw-on silencer and a four-power Schmidt and Bender scope.

A 25.2-inch-long Uzi submachine gun—the metal-butt model, still smelling of recent oiling. Five ammunition clips, thirty-two rounds in each.

Four P-15 Browning semiautomatic pistols. Each of the dozen clips cradled fifteen bullets. The big 9-millimeter slugs could punch a hole the size of a fist.

A pump-action shotgun, 10-gauge and brutally lethal to anything up to a full-grown grizzly.

And three hand grenades. Their guaranteed kill circle was a dozen yards.

The men in the brown station wagon chose their guns, loaded them expertly, and nodded.

They had their tools and detailed information about the job.

Now they could earn their money.

It was very good. So were they.

In this line of work there were very few better.

4

*T*he woods were dense. Sometimes hunters came through this thick forest during the season, but no one *lived* here. It was four miles to the nearest town—a gas station, a grocery store that doubled as a post office, and twenty-seven houses.

There were no houses out here. There was nothing but trees and an occasional clearing. In one of those a Department of Forestry fire watchtower rose sixty-eight feet into the air. A man wearing a green parka and a tan hunter's cap stood in the observation shed on top.

He wasn't a forest ranger.

They don't carry M16-A1 rifles, which are U.S. Army weapons, but he wasn't a soldier, either.

He was a watcher.

He had a big pair of binoculars on a plastic cord around his neck. He raised them to his eyes and slowly scanned the woods in each direction.

Nothing.

Walls of naked trees as far as he could see.

He didn't expect to find anyone or anything, but he did

this every ten minutes during his four-hour shift. Those were the orders.

Now he heard something and turned his head to look at the source of the sound. It was a simple hunting cabin on the far side of the clearing—twenty yards away. They were playing the radio again. The men in there did that a lot. There was no television reception out here.

The watcher had a radio, too, but not for music or news broadcasts. His set was a walkie-talkie. It rested on a table a yard from where he stood. If he saw anyone he didn't know approach the clearing, he was to use it to alert the men in the cabin.

It was much more comfortable in there. It was warmer, and there was food and soft drinks and coffee. Just as important, there were people to talk to. This was lonely duty up on the tower. It got on your nerves. After an hour or so you grew irritated and jumpy. Sometimes you started to imagine things.

It was *goddam* ridiculous, the watcher thought.

They'd been here for nineteen days, and nothing ever happened.

A deer had wandered by a week ago.

One fucking deer in almost three weeks.

Well, it would be over on Sunday.

What was that crackling noise to the left? Probably another dumb deer. Raising the binoculars to his eyes, he leaned forward and peered in the direction of the sound.

In the dense woods eighty yards away, the man who'd gotten off the train in Union Station saw him clearly in the four-power scope and pulled the trigger.

Twice.

The silencer on the rifle did its job.

So did the pair of 30.6-caliber slugs.

The man in the tower was completely surprised when they

smashed into his chest, hammering him back like twin battering rams. The front of his parka turned dark red in an instant. He swayed for a few seconds like a tree maimed by a logger's heavy ax before he crumpled to the floor.

His back was wet too.

Blood was gushing from exit holes there as well.

The pain was terrible.

Even in the searing hurt he knew what he had to do. He tried to rise to his knees. It was impossible. Desperate, he began to crawl toward the table on which the walkie-talkie rested. Like a crippled animal, he inched toward it—smearing the floor with crimson.

His outstretched hand was half a foot from the table leg. He could barely see it. Yes, he was going to make it.

Then he felt very cold.

He shuddered, clawed for the table, and died.

It was seventy-two degrees inside the heated cabin. The two men seated at the pine table were wearing T-shirts. Each had a .38 automatic pistol in the shoulder holster strapped over the thin cotton garment. One of the armed men was balding, thirty-seven years old last week. The other was barrel-chested, crew-cut and a bit younger.

The wastebasket at their feet held a dozen empty soft-drink cans, and two others sat on the table beside crumpled wax paper and the ruins of a couple of ham sandwiches. The men paid no attention to this debris, concentrating on the game cards.

They were playing Trivial Pursuit—again.

It helped pass the time on this dreary assignment.

Now a third man entered from the next room. He was twenty-eight, strong, lean, good-looking. He had sandy hair and a boyish smile. The others had kidded him that he looked like someone in an Air Force recruiting poster. It wasn't only his appearance that made them say that about the handsome Irish-American. Blair Shannon still had the youthful gung-ho spirit they'd lost somewhere over the long years.

He, too, had a .38 in a shoulder holster, and he carried an M16-A1 rifle like the one that lay beside the bloody corpse in the tower. Shannon had the next tour of duty up there. In a few moments he'd go out to the observation post to start it.

The game continued.

The balding man at the table read another question from a card.

"How many times was John Wayne nominated for an Academy Award?"

"Probably not enough," the other player answered, and reached for a soft drink.

Then Shannon spoke.

"Marcellino's still asleep. I'm gonna relieve Ed."

The players nodded, concentrating on their contest as Shannon started for the front door.

"How the hell can one son of a bitch sleep so goddam much?" the man with the crew cut asked without looking up.

"Fear," Shannon replied.

He was the youngest, but he'd learned that much.

The balding man nodded in agreement.

"Let him," he said. "As long as he wakes up to testify—"

At that moment Shannon opened the front door.

A round from the 10-gauge shotgun hit him at point-blank range like a sledgehammer. He reeled back into the room. Badly wounded, he had little left but his fierce pride. No, there was anger too.

They were enough.

His body was one mass of fire, but he could still shoot. As the two men jumped up from the table and reached for their shoulder guns, Shannon stubbornly fired out the door with his rifle.

A short burst from the six-hundred-rounds-per-minute Uzi slashed him like a butcher's cleaver. He was dead before he hit the floor. As he fell, the raiders charged in—blasting as they entered. The heavy shotgun thundered again, destroying the face of the crew-cut federal agent. Blinded and dizzy with overwhelming pain, he dropped his pistol and crumpled to his knees.

Two more bursts from the Uzi.

The other FBI man caught one in the groin and the second in the throat, cutting off a frantic curse. He doubled up, stumbled over a chair, and collapsed. His ruined body lay twitching in primeval reflex when the shotgun thundered again to end his life.

The federal agent with no face was making unintelligible sounds. They stopped when the squinty-eyed killer from the train pointed the twin 9-millimeter Brownings at his forehead and pulled the triggers.

Elapsed time from the moment Blair Shannon opened the front door: fourteen seconds.

The hit man with the shotgun reloaded, and the murder team ran through the house—firing as they moved.

Their job wasn't to slaughter FBI agents. These three had merely gotten in the way.

The assassins poured round after round at every door and wall, literally blasting the wood and fiberboard into scraps. As they charged down the hall behind a hail of bullets, a fourth federal agent dived to the floor and quickly aimed his pistol.

The shotgun and the Uzi hurled his corpse down the corridor. It stopped outside the bedroom door. There were two men inside the room. One was a grim-faced FBI agent, who swiftly pushed furniture against the portal to barricade it. The other was the terrified target of this savage assault.

Jerked from sleep by the hurricane of gunfire, he cowered in his underwear—bug-eyed with fear.

He knew that the homicidal raiders had come for him.

He knew who had sent them—and why.

Half nauseous with panic, he stared with his mouth open—unable to speak.

Outside in the hall, the kill squad stepped coolly over the corpse and resumed firing. The man with the Uzi reloaded, poured a whole clip through the door. Then two blasts from the shotgun shattered it into kindling.

The beefy man from the cabin cruiser shrugged, reached into one of the deep pockets of his knee-length jacket, and took out a grenade. As his partners stepped back, he leaned forward and reached to pull the pin.

He didn't.

Catching a glimpse of him, the tense FBI agent inside the room instantly shot him through the shoulder. The impact spun him around. Now he offered a bigger target. He screamed as the next bullet tore off his ear. He made no sound when the third slug entered his heart.

"*Shit*," the man from the airplane said softly.

There was no emotion in his voice.

It was simply a professional comment about a business error.

He began firing again with the Uzi, emptying the clip. Then he tossed it on the floor and slammed in a fresh magazine. Hosing the doorway, he crouched as he charged into the room behind the lethal barrage. The federal guard got off one more shot before the submachine gun chopped him down.

Suddenly it was quiet.

There was the man they'd come to kill.

Jerry "The Blade" Marcellino pressed his back against the bedroom wall, his eyes glassy with fear.

The coppery taste of terror filled his mouth as he tried to speak. Only gasps emerged.

He couldn't move, either. Paralyzed with dread, he stood rigid—like a butterfly corpse impaled on a pin.

The bitter-eyed man from the train stepped closer. His frown dissolved, and he smiled in malignant anticipation. This was the part of his work he liked best.

He *really* enjoyed seeing them sweat.

"We've been lookin' for you," he said venomously.

Marcellino began to shake. He tried to stop it, couldn't.

Frantic and feverish, he somehow found the strength to slide along the wall. There was a big mirror a yard from where he stopped. Reflected in the cheap glass, his sallow face was even more distorted with desperation.

"So you want to be a witness?" the grinning assassin taunted.

Whimpering, Marcellino turned away in hopeless dread.

"Okay, witness *this,*" his tormentor ordered, and pressed the muzzle of the pistol in his right hand against the back of Marcellino's skull. The gunman waited for several seconds, relishing every moment.

"Come on, will you?" the hit man in the blue business suit urged impatiently.

The man from the train sighed and squeezed the trigger. A sheet of blood and bits of brain and bone splattered the mirror. The remains of the late Jerry Marcellino tumbled onto the green shag rug. Then the sadist who'd killed him shot the corpse between the eyes—just to make sure.

"It's over," the other hit man said. "Let's go."

The federal agent sprawled near the door moaned. Mortally wounded by seven rounds from the Uzi, he wasn't quite dead yet. He would be in a few minutes, but the man from the train didn't want to wait.

You didn't hang around one extra second after a hit.

You didn't leave any living witnesses, either.

"Shit," the man in the business suit said, and finished the job with another burst from the submachine gun.

"*Now* it's over," the man from the train said cheerfully, and then they left. The gritty singing of Willie Nelson was pouring from the radio in the front room as they walked out of the cabin.

5

It was a hunter's moon.

Full ... strong ... bright.

The woods were dark, but the clearing in the forest was illuminated by the headlights of a dozen police cars.

And two coroner's vans.

The flashing gumball-machine lamps atop the law enforcement teams' vehicles rotated like hysterical lighthouse beacons. In addition to the state and local police cruisers, there were three other cars that bore no official markings or moving beams.

There was no quiet in the woods this night. Men were speaking on two-way radios. Others talked as they stalked the clearing in pairs, their faces grim and their weapons drawn. The uniformed cops carrying the body bags from the house said nothing. They had cursed when they'd first seen the bloody corpses. Now they had no more words.

Tight-lipped with shock and anger, they were silent as they loaded the body bags into the vans. The white-uniformed coroner's men didn't speak, either. They were used to victims of car crashes and hunting accidents. This was their first massacre.

It was very bright inside the ravaged cabin. Laboratory technicians and photographers had set up powerful lamps on metal tripods. The lab men were searching for evidence, going over each room inch by inch. The photographers were shooting their last pictures of the scene of the crime.

Shattered doors.

Blasted walls.

Dark crimson stains and smears almost everywhere.

Scores of shell casings littered the floors, and there were chalk marks where the bodies had been found. One corpse was still in the front room in a plastic bag.

A gray-haired man in his mid-fifties sat on the floor beside it. His eyes were swollen, and the tears on his wide, anguished face had not yet dried. He wore a gray civilian suit, not a police uniform. Clipped to the outer breast pocket of his jacket was an FBI identification card.

The name on it explained why he grieved so deeply.

He was Harry Shannon.

The handsome young agent who'd caught the shotgun blast at the front door was his son.

It was the corpse of Blair Shannon in the body bag a yard away.

As Harry Shannon looked at the plastic shroud numbly, another man wearing the FBI card approached him. The father's pain was almost tangible, and the other agent spoke cautiously.

"Harry?"

Shannon didn't seem to hear him.

"Harry, they wanna take him out."

Shannon glanced up and blinked. There was a remote look in his reddened eyes—as if he didn't quite know where he was. He turned to stare at the bag again. After a few seconds he spread the top eighteen inches open to study his firstborn's face. More tears ran down Harry Shannon's face. Then he drew the plastic together again.

The other federal agent nodded. Two uniformed Illinois State Police stepped forward with a litter. They loaded the body bag onto it carefully as Shannon spoke again.

"*Twenty-seven* years," he said bitterly. "In twenty-seven years of this shit I never got a scratch . . . Jesus Christ!"

A wave of hurt contorted his face again. The primal emotion of a mourning father choked his throat, but he forced himself to stifle the sobs. He had to maintain his control.

The suffering left his features.

There was something very different in his eyes.

It was in his voice, too.

"I want a list," he said in a tone as cold and hard as a bayonet. "A complete list of everybody in Witness Protection who knew where we were holding Marcellino."

"Right."

"And anyone else who *could* have known," Shannon continued. "Any goddam one else—from the Commissioner to the D.A. or higher."

Harry Shannon was beyond shock now. The veteran FBI operative still hurt, but another emotion was even stronger.

Vengeance for a murdered son.

Shannon rose to his feet. He looked squarely into the eyes of the other FBI agent, who stood a bare yard away.

"They're *dead*, Mike," he announced. "I'm going to get the mothers who set this up—every one of them. *Whoever* they are . . . *whatever* it takes, they're all *dead*."

It was an almost impossible task, the other agent thought. At least fifty people in the FBI and a dozen in Illinois law enforcement knew about this "safe house." There could be others too.

A clerk or secretary who eavesdropped on a phone call.

A minor Department of Justice paper-pusher who was being blackmailed.

A wiretapper hired by the multimillionaire ganglord against whom Marcellino was to testify.

The money-hungry girlfriend of a cop or federal agent who talked too much.

There was practically no chance that the cunning traitor would ever be identified, the agent thought. He couldn't say that to the grieving father, though, so Special Agent Michael Flynn merely nodded sympathetically.

He watched Harry Shannon stare down at the chalk marks that ringed the place where his firstborn son had died. Then Shannon wiped the tears from his cheeks, and the two FBI men made their way out to their car.

The coroner's vans were just leaving.

Shannon stared at them intently until they were out of sight.

"Every one of them," he promised.

He didn't utter another word on the long drive back to Chicago.

He was making his plan.

6

Three days later.

Nine hundred and eighty miles away.

A sunny afternoon in the rolling hills of rural North Carolina.

Warm . . . lazy . . . peaceful.

Suddenly the quiet was smashed. The grinding thunder of a heavy motorcycle shattered the serenity of the balmy morning.

The large cycle was charging down the country highway at top speed, twenty-five miles an hour above the limit. The leather-jacketed driver was no law-busting Hell's Angel. He was a uniformed state trooper, pushing his machine for everything it could give.

He wasn't pursuing some reckless speeder or fleeing criminal.

He was the one being chased.

No, *hunted*.

A battered mud-splattered jeep raced right behind him. It was only seventy yards back, moving like a juggernaut. The man at the wheel—unshaven, muscular, and tough-faced in a hard but handsome way—was totally determined to stop that motorcycle.

And the policeman.

At any risk or cost.

The peace of the countryside was over. This was war. The fact that the weapons were wheeled didn't matter. Both the man on the motorcycle and the driver of the jeep knew that they were locked in naked combat—a battle without quarter.

Now the jeep was closing the gap. The man at the wheel didn't look very dangerous. But he was. Though dressed in soiled jeans and a worn denim jacket, he drove with a skill far beyond that of any local farmer. He guided the jeep with a ruthless ferocity. He had total control of the vehicle, as if the machine were an extension of his powerful arms.

The road was his.

He could not be defeated here.

Recognizing this, the trooper suddenly swerved his cycle off the concrete and into the forest. He was an excellent driver too. The larger vehicle couldn't follow into these woods.

It did.

The hunter in the jeep twisted his steering wheel in a sharp turn, literally muscling it at a right angle toward the trees. Two tires lifted off the ground, and the acrid stench of burning rubber filled the air as the hard-eyed driver fought for control.

He won.

He hurled the jeep into the woods like a tank. The motorcycle was out of sight, but that didn't discourage him at all. Even as a boy, Mark Kaminski never gave up easily. He certainly wasn't about to do so now.

The jeep bucked and snarled as it struggled through the heavy underbrush, ripping through bushes and bouncing over rocks as Kaminski zigzagged between the trees. He wasn't bothered by the fact that there was no trail. He carved out his own path, ignoring the branches that whipped his face.

A tree limb slashed at his forehead, and blood seeped from an inch-long wound. Another branch whipsawed a gash on his cheek. Those cuts didn't matter. All he could think was that his prey was getting away. He couldn't even hear it anymore.

On the far side of the forest the motorcycle burst from the woods. Smiling triumphantly, the uniformed rider drove it across an untilled field toward an old barn. With its sagging doors wide-open and its weathered walls blotched with age, the weary structure was obviously long abandoned.

But it was part of a farm, and that meant there was a road not far beyond. The cyclist guided his machine around the barn to find that rural road. In a few minutes he'd be miles away.

As the motorcycle swept around the aged structure the jeep surged out of the line of trees. It bounced across the rough terrain of the untilled field in stubborn pursuit. Every second—every yard—counted.

Kaminski computed and decided. He knifed the jeep between the battered doors and roared right into the barn at full speed. It was like threading a needle at seventy miles an hour, but he did it.

The jeep smashed into a heap of egg crates, hurling them out of the way like matchboxes. Then it slammed into a bale of dry hay, blasting it into a cloud. For a moment he couldn't see.

But he wouldn't slow down.

Now the jeep ran into a heap of old farm implements. The impact knocked an ax into the air, throwing it into a wall where it stuck—shuddering. The wooden shaft of a pitchfork snapped in two. The end with the twisted steel prongs crashed into a half-empty drum of diesel fuel, pouring spouts of petroleum over the floor.

The jeep spun on the slick surface. Handling the vehicle like a racing driver, Kaminski did not fight the momentum. He used it, working the wheel skillfully to keep control. The jeep turned in a complete circle and roared on out the other end of the barn.

He saw the motorcycle one hundred yards ahead. It was bumping over the dirt and gravel of a twisting, unpaved road. Five seconds later he saw something else.

If the barn was abandoned, this farm wasn't. A big tractor was crawling noisily from a field. It moved directly toward the unpaved road.

With barely a yard to spare the trooper raced by it a moment before the huge John Deere blocked the route like a landslide.

Kaminski pounded his fist on the jeep's horn, scourging the morning air with long bursts of ugly sound. The farmer on the tractor paid no attention to the urgent appeals. He had the bigger machine—the power that comes with more pounds of moving metal. Why should he get out of the way for some damn trespasser? Might made right, and weight made fate. Those were the facts of life.

The jeep was hurtling closer. The farmhand didn't even glance at it. If the fool in the smaller vehicle wanted to commit suicide, that was his business.

The jeep horn snarled again and again.

Fifty yards.

Forty yards.

Thirty.

Kaminski didn't swear or blink. Recognizing the crude arrogance of the man on the tractor, he swung the jeep in a sharp right turn and raced off the road. The tractor had cost him precious time. Churning up dust, the jeep bulled ahead on a course parallel to the motorcycle. But the gap was bigger now.

More than two hundred yards.

And the motorcycle was getting farther ahead by the second.

It thundered off the farm road onto a paved highway, and the trooper poured on the speed.

Three hundred yards.

There were other vehicles rolling down the highway—trucks and cars moving steadily in both directions. They'd make it harder to catch the cycle.

Kaminski pulled the jeep to a screeching stop at the edge of the road and saw the motorcycle getting smaller and smaller in the distance. He had only one chance. He grabbed it.

Jamming his gas pedal to the floor, he barreled boldly across both lanes of moving traffic. Stunned and shaken, the drivers of a dozen other vehicles hit their brakes and frantically twisted their wheels. Their cars and trucks slid and dodged in desperate evasive action as they sweated to avoid fiery death. A small Toyota whiplashed off the road into a clump of saplings.

Kaminski didn't see any of that. He was staring intently at the receding motorcycle. A moment after it vanished, he drove the jeep across the rough field back into the woods. Handling his vehicle like a masterful madman, he speared it between the trees—missing some and glancing off others as it bucked and bounced ahead wildly.

It was like riding an unbroken bronco.

Bone-jarring . . . dangerous . . . unpredictable.

Twice the metal steed nearly turned over.

Again and again he was almost thrown out by the impact of the brutal collisions.

Only his animal strength, swift reflexes, and fierce determination kept him in the jolting, heaving vehicle. Any reasonable person could see that the jeep couldn't take much more, but thirty-seven-year-old Mark Kaminski wasn't feeling reasonable. Determined to track down his prey, he fought the machine and the forest with everything he had.

A mile away the sweat-drenched trooper swung his motorcycle onto the shoulder of the highway and stopped. He was panting as he looked back. He'd never had an experience anything like this. The man in the jeep had to be crazy—a homicidal maniac, he thought. He should have shot the goddam lunatic, or at least blown out one of the madman's tires.

Gasping and furious, the motorcyclist looked back.

There was no sign of the jeep.

He'd lost the psycho, but this was no time to take chances. The crazy bastard might come booming down the highway at any moment. The trooper accelerated as he turned off into a dirt road. A minute later he saw a steep hill. It was scarred by tracks of other cyclists who'd used it to prove their cross-country and climbing skills.

The tire marks all went up. The others had made it over the top, and he would too. He had a bull of a machine and the experience to handle it well. He brushed the beads of perspiration from his brow, smiled confidently, and twisted his throttle to full power.

The cycle had plenty of momentum as it reached the steep incline. He handled it perfectly, working his way up steadily. His engine strained and made harsh grating sounds. But it kept moving him up toward the top.

When he was almost at the crest, he looked back again.

No jeep.

He'd lost the lunatic.

Then he turned around to face forward as the cycle reached the top.

His eyes bulged and his jaw fell in shock.

The mud-splattered jeep was forty yards away.

It was hurling right at him.

When the gap was only fifteen yards, Kaminski slammed on his brakes. The abrupt drop in speed shoved him forward. He pushed back with all his strength to keep his face from smashing into the windshield.

The jeep's heavy bumper crashed into the motorcycle's front wheel. The cycle and its uniformed rider flew back, twisting and spinning as they hurtled through the air. Pieces of the bike exploded in every direction as the ruined machine slammed into the ground halfway down the side of the hill. The trooper's body fell a few yards away.

It didn't move.

The jeep was still rolling toward the edge. In a moment it would tumble off the hill too. Kaminski fought it to a shuddering halt scant inches from disaster. Half of each front tire was over the edge.

He'd come *that* close to losing.

Maybe dying.

Still, he was calm as he got out of the jeep and looked down. A small, steely smile showed on his face. He was content. The savage little war was finished. He'd won.

Eyeing the wrecked cycle and the body nearby, he wondered whether the man was dead. Kaminski had killed before, but he hoped that this man was still alive.

Kaminski wasn't finished with him yet.

7

Half an hour and twenty-three miles later.

Barrett, North Carolina—population 4,610.

Mid-afternoon traffic was light as Kaminski guided the dusty jeep down the main street. When he reached the center of the small town, he turned left at the Veterans Monument and drove a block to a two-story building of red brick. There was a weathered brass plate screwed to the wall beside the front door.

SHERIFF'S OFFICE.

Kaminski parked behind a police car, slid from the jeep, and walked around to pull out his sullen passenger. The motorcyclist was wearing handcuffs. His uniform jacket was ripped, his face swollen, and his eyes bitter with hate. He scowled as Kaminski shoved him toward the entrance of the building.

"Inside, *Officer*," Kaminski ordered bluntly, in a voice that wasn't the least bit Southern.

It was edged with a foreign accent.

Central or Eastern Europe.

He pushed his captive through the doorway. Barrett wasn't

a rich town. Every piece of furniture and equipment in
the sheriff's office was at least ten years old—strictly
functional.

There were two men inside. A curly-haired deputy was
working the police radio. Another young deputy—lanky and
earnest—sat hunt-and-peck, typing a report about a stolen
horse. They both looked up as Kaminski entered, pushing
the handcuffed trooper ahead of him.

"Hot damn!" the younger deputy exulted.

"So you got the bastard," the other deputy said ad-
miringly.

"In the act," Kaminski replied.

"*Bullshit.*" The battered cyclist sneered. "Hell, I was
just goin' to a costume party."

"At four in the afternoon in a trooper's uniform?" the
deputy at the typewriter asked. "Where'd you nail him,
Sheriff?"

"Route 74," Kaminski answered. "He stopped somebody for driving too fast . . . was gonna let 'em off for fifty
bucks."

"He's crazy," the prisoner insisted. "*They* stopped *me* to
ask directions."

"What about the money?" the muscular sheriff asked as
he strode to the old-fashioned water cooler and filled a
paper cup.

"That was their idea. They offered it."

"To help you buy a new costume—something in stripes.
Book him," Kaminski ordered.

"What for?" the fake trooper demanded.

"Impersonating a police officer . . . resisting arrest . . .
speeding . . . reckless driving . . . reckless endangerment . . .
fraud . . . lying to the sheriff . . . and having a big, dirty
mouth."

Then Kaminski put down a 38-caliber pistol beside the typewriter.

"And carrying an unlicensed weapon," he added.

"This is a frame-up. I want a lawyer!" the surly crook said loudly.

"You'd better get two," the curly-haired deputy advised.

Enraged, the larcenous "trooper" tried to kick Kaminski in the groin. The deputies grinned as their boss stepped aside, picked up the criminal as if he was a doll, and slammed him into a wooden chair. One arm broke off the chair under the impact.

"Better add destroying public property," Kaminski told his grinning assistants. "I'm going now. If you need me, I'll be at home."

"You'll be seeing me!" the furious con man vowed.

"In four or five years," Kaminski replied as he pointed to the door that led to the cells.

"We'll take care of this turkey, Sheriff," the lanky deputy promised.

Then he tugged the glowering crook to his feet.

"So you wanna play policeman?" he asked. "Okay with me. Come on, Deputy Dawg."

The fake trooper was cursing as Kaminski strode from the building.

8

Kaminski should have been smiling as he drove away from police headquarters.

He should have been happy after his victory.

But his face was impassive, and there was discontent in his eyes.

Something was gnawing at him—inside.

It had been for a long time. He wasn't one of those men who doesn't understand or won't face what is bothering him. Mark Kaminski had known himself since he was twelve years old, and he knew exactly what the trouble was.

That wasn't enough.

There was still the question of what he should or could do about it. He'd been trying to answer that for many months. He thought about it again and again every day, and even more in the stillness of the Carolina nights.

He hadn't discussed it with anyone in town. Kaminski was a private person who dealt with his own problems. He'd always been able to handle them before. Endowed with a mind as quick and strong as his body, he was a lot smarter than ninety-five percent of the people he met, and few of them realized that. The idea that muscular men were not too bright was still a popular assumption.

This is a nice town, he thought as he guided the jeep up a tree-lined street. The pace was easy, and people were decent. Crime here was less common and less vicious than in the noisy, dirty, crowded city he'd left. No cop had been killed in this county for years.

The area was so old-fashioned that people still respected laws and lawmen. A quartet of eighth-grade children on bicycles waved and called out in greeting as the jeep passed them.

"Hi, Sheriff!" they chorused.

Kaminski gestured and tried to smile back. Even though he liked these friendly, clean-cut kids, it took an effort. There was no real enthusiasm in his reflex response. With his unsolved problem he was rarely enthusiastic these days.

Ten minutes later he reached his home on the edge of town. It was a small, freshly painted frame house with a neatly trimmed front lawn. He cut the grass every week himself, and he took care of the rosebushes. It wasn't just because he liked roses. He enjoyed working with his hands.

He slowed the jeep, nosed it up the driveway, and parked ten feet from the immaculate garage. Then he got out to walk wearily toward the front door. The evening paper from the county seat was lying on the grass nearby. He scooped it up and strode to the door.

He paused for a moment before he entered, wondering what he'd find inside.

Last night . . . last week . . . last month had been hard.

Maybe it would be better tonight. Maybe not.

Kaminski nodded, squared his big shoulders, and entered his home. The front door opened directly into the living room. Comfortable but visibly inexpensive furniture filled the right half of the room, and the left was dominated by an assortment of first-class bodybuilding equipment.

One of her favorite LPs was spinning on the record player. The Haydn symphony blasted from the stereo speakers like an artillery barrage. Turned up to maximum sound, the surging sounds of a hundred and five musicians were almost deafening.

Why was it so ferociously loud?

The answer was visible on top of one speaker.

Two empty bottles of beer.

She'd started earlier than usual.

"Amy? Amy?" he called out as he turned down the volume.

There was no answer. Where was she?

Some twenty feet away, Amy Kaminski was busy in the kitchen. An extremely attractive brunette in her late twenties, she wore a sleeveless cotton dress that didn't conceal her shapely figure. The well-conditioned muscles on her arms signaled that she, too, used the bodybuilding gear regularly.

She wasn't working on her body now. She was working on a large round cake that she'd just taken from the oven. Wielding a rubber spatula, she was clumsily applying thick, uneven layers of dark chocolate frosting.

As Kaminski stepped into the doorway she picked up a bottle of beer and took a long swallow. Then she took another. Now he knew what was coming. She was half drunk again, and she wasn't finished. It was going to be another one of those nights.

"We having a party?" he asked.

"Of course! I'm glad you're home early to join in the celebration."

She looked around for a place to put down the bottle, tossed it toward the open garbage pail, and missed. The bottle broke into four pieces. She ignored that and resumed smearing icing on the cake.

"Is the party just us, or are we having company?" he asked.

She drank from another open beer bottle before she replied.

"Just us, Sheriff. Who else in this wonderful metropolis could appreciate the glory of this anniversary?" she challenged bitterly.

She dabbed on more icing, studied her work, and heaved the spatula over her shoulder toward the sink. It landed on a pile of fresh laundry, splatting everything with gobs of dark chocolate.

"What are we celebrating, Amy?"

"Our fifth anniversary!" she announced harshly. "Five horrible years in exile in this desert."

"Come on, it's a nice, friendly town."

She glared, began patting down the icing with a bare hand.

"Five damn years in a dreary place with no symphony orchestra . . . no art gallery or museum . . . no decent restaurant. And nobody who talks about anything but the crops and the weather!" she accused, smacking the cake for emphasis.

He shrugged and took a beer from the refrigerator.

"It's not forever," he reasoned.

"The *hell* it's not!"

"Let it go," he urged as he opened the bottle.

"You could still be with the Bureau! We could still be in New York, living a civilized life. You could have fought it. You didn't have to quit, Mark!"

He finally lost his patience.

"You're lucky they let me," he told her bluntly. "If it

had gone to trial, I'd have lost and they'd have booted me out. Then I couldn't even have gotten this job."

He had enough of this all too familiar argument.

Maybe changing the subject might help.

"What's for dinner?"

"Just this," she replied, and began to spray letters of imitation whipped cream on the cake.

"We're gonna get fat," he warned with a small smile.

"We're already fat . . . fat in the head. Fat like the cows they raise around here. You know what a cow's biggest contribution is?"

When he shook his head, she raised the cake so that he could see what she'd written on it.

One word.

Four letters and an exclamation point.

SHIT!

Before he could say anything, she threw the cake right at him. He dodged effortlessly, and it splattered across the wall. He eyed the mess coolly and turned to face her.

"You shouldn't drink and bake," he advised wryly.

She stared at him angrily before she gulped another mouthful of beer. After a few moments she began to smile. Then she laughed. She loved this strong, caring man and his odd sense of humor.

"You're crazy," she told him affectionately.

Now they were both laughing at the absurdity of the situation. He was still chuckling as he ran a finger through the mess on the wall and tasted it.

"Not *bad*," he told her, "but your tossed salad is better."

She didn't mind the bad joke. The man was good, and the flush of love and beer made her warm and wanting. She pulled the cotton dress up over her head, dropped it on the floor.

"Why don't we forget about dinner for a little while?" she suggested.

"Good idea," he agreed, and took her hand.

The kitchen clock showed five minutes after five.

They didn't return to the kitchen to eat until half past eight.

9

The elegant sounds of Mozart's Concerto Number 20 filled the dimly lit living room. The volume level on the record player was low, but Kaminski savored every note. He still had the ears and eyes and hair-trigger reflexes of a nineteen-year-old athlete.

He was sitting on the couch thinking. His drowsy wife's head rested on his lap. Sated by lovemaking and half sedated by beer, she sprawled over the length of the couch—nude. The anger was gone from her face now, and her full figure was the stuff of artists' dreams. She was a beautiful young woman.

Thirsty after their hours of carnal connection, she had started another bottle of beer. Her flesh was warm, but the half-empty glass container in her hand was still cold. As she drifted toward sleep he gently took the bottle from her fingers and set it on the table.

Barely awake, she sighed and smiled. For the moment she was again the serene and radiant woman he'd wed. It wouldn't last too long, he reflected. She'd be bitter again when she awoke to face the realities of the life she so deeply loathed. At best, numbing herself with intense physical pleasure and alcohol was a temporary escape.

She sighed softly again as she floated into the safety of a dream. He slipped out from under her, easily lifted her in his powerful arms, and carried her back to their bed. He laid her down carefully, pulled the rumpled cover over that remarkable body, and kissed her lips lightly. She smiled again in her sleep.

When Kaminski returned to the living room, he changed the record before half filling a snifter with Martell's superb Cordon Bleu cognac. As he sipped the subtle fire he recalled how she'd driven ninety-five miles in the searing July heat to buy this bottle of his favorite brandy for his birthday.

You couldn't find it anywhere in this county, he thought, brooding as the sounds of Isaac Stern's violin soared from the twin speakers. The fine cognac itself wasn't important— except as a symbol. It represented all the limitations of existence here.

She was right.

They were slowing down in this placid backwater.

It wasn't that Barrett was a bad place.

It just wasn't enough for Mark and Amy Kaminski.

There was no stimulation . . . no challenge. Everything and everyone were half-speed and narrow-gauged—like the obsolete steam locomotives that struggled up the Andes.

Even the crime was minor league. Catching a motorcyclist who tricked gullible farmers out of fifty dollars was the most exciting thing that had happened to Sheriff Kaminski in a year. The biggest case in the seventeen months before that had involved a pair of buck-toothed brothers who'd stolen four pickup trucks.

It had been a lot different during his decade with the Bureau. The FBI had recognized him as a big-league talent, so he was given tough and important criminals to stop. The elite teams that he'd been assigned to had fought it out with major gangs and smashed them. They'd shattered a Sovblock spy ring stealing military secrets in California's Silicon Valley, and they'd ended the Wyatt mob's interstate hijacking operation in a hurricane of bullets near Newark Airport. None of the seven hoodlums who survived would be out of jail before 1995.

Kaminski's pulse quickened as he relived the demolition of The Four Cousins "laundry" operations that handled $280 million a year for Atlantic City casino skimmers and East Coast dope dealers. The cunning Cousins used trigger-happy Colombian "cowboys" to escort their cash shipments. Heavy firepower—vicious little MAC10 submachine guns less than a foot long that spit over a thousand rounds a minute—had been their trademark.

The Cousins' "vault" had been a warehouse in the Queens section of New York City. It looked nondescript from the street, but there were reinforced steel doors and a sandbagged gun position that was manned around the clock. Attack dogs and closed-circuit television cameras added to the defense. The cash was moved in and out in an armor-plated Mercedes built for an African dictator who'd been assassinated before he could take delivery.

Kaminski had come up with the idea for how to break into the gangsters' fort. Wearing a flak jacket under the uniform of a Sanitation Department worker, he'd driven up one freezing January morning in a garbage truck equipped with a snowplow. Suddenly twisting the steering wheel sharply, he'd rammed the gas pedal to the floor to crash through the garage door. The snowplow ripped it open as if it were a sardine can, and the self-propelled juggernaut smashed in before the alarms could sound.

The noise of the demolition and the ringing bells brought
the Colombian guards running. They stopped when Kaminski
rolled out of the truck and hurled the concussion grenades.
The blasts sent them reeling, blood jetting from their ears
and noses. Three carloads of other FBI men ended the
attack, disarming most of the dazed gunmen before they
could fire a shot. One stubborn hoodlum got off a burst
before Kaminski dropped him with bullets through both
kneecaps.

The wounded thug's lawyer had ranted about sadism, but
the Bureau had understood. Maybe he wouldn't walk right
for a long time, but that was a lot better than lying on a slab
in the morgue. To Kaminski's surprise, a New York police
reporter who rarely wrote anything favorable about the cops
had pointed that out in print.

Only one of the Cousins had been captured in the warehouse. Two others had been arrested in their luxurious
homes. Released on bail of $1 million each, they'd fled the
country. That hadn't surprised Kaminski at all, he remembered as he savored the excellent cognac. While the
inexperienced U.S. magistrate who set the bail considered
$1 million a huge sum, it meant little to the enormously rich
Cousins.

It didn't really anger Kaminski.

He hadn't lost his temper until the Gilbert case.

That had destroyed his career.

The jangling of the telephone jerked him back to today.
He seized the instrument immediately, hoping that the noise
hadn't awakened her. He listened for a moment, heard
nothing from the bedroom.

It was all right.

She was still sleeping.

He nodded, put down the snifter of Martell, and raised
the phone to his ear.

"Hello? Hello? Mark?" a familiar voice asked.

"Yeah?"

"Mark? It's Harry Shannon."

Kaminski reached for the cognac and sipped before he replied.

"How's it going, Harry? It's been a long time."

Three goddam years.

"I've got a problem," Shannon announced bluntly.

"Uh-huh."

"A big problem. I have to talk to you."

"Talk," Kaminski told him.

"*Not* on the phone."

"It's all I've got time for."

"Things not so good?" the FBI agent asked, testing.

"I've seen better days."

"Want to see them again, Mark?"

Why would Shannon call him? He had the whole damn Bureau to call on. It had to be something tricky—probably dirty too. But Harry Shannon was always Mr. Clean.

"What have you got in mind?" Kaminski asked warily.

"Meet me and I'll tell you."

What the hell!

Whatever it was, it wouldn't be dull like life here.

"Okay, Harry. Where and when?"

10

High-tech.

Not quite Star Wars but definitely state-of-the-art.

The art was war. The electronics equipment that lined the softly lit corridor was the latest U.S. Army ground radar, low-altitude antiaircraft and missile scanners and sophisticated monitoring hardware that could pick up a man's footstep or body heat at one thousand yards.

It wasn't an exhibit.

It was all being used.

Every console was being operated by highly skilled men and women in Army uniform. Every radar screen and computer display panel was being watched intently by experts who quietly reported to the command post CO via small microphones connected to the headsets they all wore.

A battle was being fought up above this massive steel-and-concrete bunker. The warriors in the underground shelter were directing it—coolly and surely. They were professionals. They didn't have to see or hear the missiles flying, shells and mortar rounds bursting, and rapid-fire guns spewing destruction. They were waging the new kind of war of the eighties—well.

Shannon led the way down the long passage. Following a yard behind, Kaminski eyed the strange scene curiously. It hadn't been anything like this in Nam.

"The Bureau picks odd places to meet," he said wryly.

Shannon shook his head.

"Not the Bureau—*me*. The general here's an old buddy I soldiered with in Korea," he announced.

They walked on until they reached a metal-sheathed door set flush into the left side of the tunnel wall. No keyhole, no knob to grasp. The closed-circuit video camera overhead confirmed that this was a security area that no one entered unless somebody inside approved.

Kaminski wondered what was behind the barrier. The black sign stenciled on the door gave no clue. All it said was B-81 AUTHORIZED PERSONNEL ONLY.

Then Shannon spoke again.

"This is my own deal, Mark. If you want out, say it now."

So it wasn't an official Bureau operation.

Should have figured that, Kaminski thought.

No one in the FBI hierarchy would offer him *anything*. They wanted to forget about former Special Agent Mark Kaminski, who had broken the cardinal rule . . . committed the unpardonable sin.

He had embarrassed the Bureau.

Kaminski studied the door for several seconds.

"I'd like to hear your offer, Harry."

Shannon took out his FBI identity card and held it toward the camera. There was a low, whirring sound as someone inside adjusted the lens for a close-up, and then the heavy door opened.

Three of the walls of the chamber were covered with

metal shelves that held thousands of videotapes. The fourth was invisible behind racks crammed with videocassette players and an assortment of television sets—some standard nineteen-inch models and others equipped with projectors that delivered much bigger pictures.

There was a pretty black woman in the room. She wore horn-rimmed glasses that did not reduce her good looks, and the single silver bar of a first lieutenant adorned each shoulder of her uniform jacket.

"May I have your Social Security number, please?" she asked crisply.

"058-33-7199," Shannon answered.

She consulted her clipboard and pointed to one of the nineteen-inch sets.

"Your tape's ready to roll. Do you know how to run a VCR, Mr. Shannon?"

When he nodded, she walked to the far end of the room and sat down, facing the door. She knew this chamber's security rules. Whatever was on this cassette was none of her business. She put on a headset, flicked the controls on another machine, and saw pictures of battle. She immediately resumed taking notes.

Shannon and Kaminski placed two of the scoop-bottom plastic chairs in front of their TV screen, and the older man punched the start button.

They saw a man's face—thin, lined by years, and coldly arrogant. His expression was one of naked power.

The close-up filled the entire screen.

Kaminski had seen him before. So had millions of other Americans. Hundreds of them were no longer alive. His authority wasn't merely that of enormous wealth. His power was the ultimate one—of life and death.

He recognized no government.

He accepted no law but his own. He had his own banks

and his own army. Anyone he couldn't intimidate or buy, he had his soldiers destroy. During the past twenty years, more than thirteen hundred corpses confirmed his ruthless determination and vicious savagery.

His law was simple.

Pay or die.

Proud of the fear and power, he liked the name that the media had given him.

"The Emperor," Kaminski said.

Now someone off-camera spoke.

"Mr. Patrovita, I'd like you to explain something."

Nothing showed in the ganglord's piercing black eyes.

He'd been questioned by other prosecutors and crime commissions and legislative committees.

They'd gotten publicity—but not Patrovita.

None of them had hurt The Emperor at all.

He had the best attorneys and politicians money could buy—and an icy contempt for the pitiful efforts to trap him.

"Mr. Patrovita, you deny any illicit income or connection with organized crime," the polished voice continued. "You reported income of $79,000 last year."

The voice was familiar.

Kaminski leaned forward.

"On that income, Mr. Patrovita, you somehow supported a seven-bedroom mansion here in Chicago, a hunting lodge on two hundred acres in Wisconsin, a three-bedroom condominium in Florida, four Cadillacs..."

At this point the TV newsman shifted to a wider shot, and Kaminski saw another man. It was the questioner. He was dressed in full Ivy League uniform of gray flannel suit, button-down Oxford cloth blue shirt, and striped silk tie.

The son of a bitch had chosen blue because it was a "good" color for television, Kaminski guessed accurately.

He'd do that.

Kaminski knew the interrogator—too well.

He was shrewd and aggressive. His build was medium, but his ambitions were gigantic.

"And a life-style that makes Ted Turner look like a derelict. How do you do that on $79,000 a year?"

Kaminski couldn't wait. His hand punched the freeze button on the VCR—leaving the questioner's face dominating the center of the screen.

"It's that bastard Baxter," Kaminski said.

"I know," Shannon replied.

"What the hell is he doing in Chicago?"

"Special prosecutor."

"Special *creep*. Everything by the book," Kaminski said bitterly.

"That's the way lawyers are, Mark."

"Some of them are human. Marvin Baxter is just righteous. That pious bastard never gave me a chance."

"Mark, you brought in a prisoner with half the damn bones in his body broken. He was a walking fracture. No, a crawling one. Looked like a train had hit him."

"He got off easy."

"For God's sake, Mark, any prosecutor would have gone after you for wrecking that man."

Kaminski shook his head.

"Not man—*animal*," he corrected. "Remember the case?"

"I remember."

"Not the way I do. You didn't see the body in thirteen pieces. An eleven-year-old girl—raped and tortured and mutilated with a saw-toothed knife—while she was still conscious."

Shannon took out and lit a cigarette.

"He was a sick person, Mark."

"That's what his father's fancy shrinks and high-priced lawyers said," Kaminski remembered. "Just a poor, disturbed boy whose daddy went to Yale with the mayor. Boy? He was twenty-two, a full-grown monster.''

"It was the times," Ryan said. "The public didn't like cops then—especially rough ones."

"No, Baxter was making a name and sucking up to the mayor. He wanted to look like a saint to the press. I tried to tell him what really happened, how this misunderstood rich kid came at me with the same blade he chopped her up with. He knew karate, too, you know."

The older man puffed on the cigarette.

"What did Baxter say?"

"Excessive force. What are you supposed to do when a murderer tries to rip your guts out with an eight-inch blade—ask for his autograph?"

"That was five years ago," Shannon reminded. "I want to talk *today*."

Kaminski refused to change the subject.

"So the butcher goes to a mental hospital for a couple of years of long talks and fingerpainting lessons before they decide he's cured—and my career is destroyed. Resign or be prosecuted. *That's* what Baxter said!"

"If it's any consolation, Mark, he's giving Patrovita a hard time too."

Shannon hit the play button, and the tape rolled again.

Another close-up of The Emperor.

He looked bored as he answered Baxter's sarcastic question.

"This is old stuff. I bought those houses cheap. We've been through the whole thing with the IRS about four times. Why don't you talk to my accountants?"

"You deny that you're worth millions?" the prosecutor persisted.

"Actually, I've got a lot of debts."

"To whom?"

"Old friends."

"Like Carl Rocca and Swede Swenson?" Baxter challenged.

"I got a lot of friends," the monarch of the Midwestern rackets answered evenly.

"Are Swenson and Rocca just friends, or are they also business associates?" Baxter demanded as he reached for the FBI folders containing their criminal records.

Patrovita glanced at his gray-haired attorney and saw the two-hundred-dollar-an-hour lawyer adjust the knot of his seventy-dollar tie. That was the signal.

"I don't feel well, Mr. Baxter. I got a heart problem, you know."

"Answer the question."

"My doctor says I gotta avoid stress. I plead the Fifth Amendment."

The scene on the TV screen changed abruptly. Now Baxter was questioning another man—a decade younger than Patrovita. He was in his mid-forties, burly, and coarse-featured. In contrast to Patrovita's low-key attire he wore a flashy pin-striped suit, a tailor-made yellow silk shirt, and an eye-catching brocade tie. His big feet were shod in six-hundred-dollar boots, and the big gold watch on his right wrist was a ninety-four-hundred-dollar Rolex—the model favored by Arab princes.

Vain . . . vulgar . . . smug.

It was written all over him.

"Mr. Rocca—" Baxter began.

He didn't get to finish.

"Listen." Rocca broke in loudly in a gravelly voice. "I'm a busy guy and you're wastin' my time. I'm takin' the Fifth on whatever phony questions you're asking. I got a lot of rights. I don't have to put up with this harassment. This ain't Russia, mister."

"Thank you for the lesson in constitutional law," Baxter

answered archly. "We all appreciate your reminder about our inalienable rights and—"

Shannon turned off the machine.

"Carl Rocca," he identified. "Carl the Boot. Used to stomp people when he was just muscle on the way up. Killed his first man at seventeen. Still likes to kick men—or women—in the face, if he gets the chance."

"What's his connection with Lu Patrovita?" Kaminski asked.

"He's the undertaker. Somebody bothers The Emperor and The Boot buries them in Lake Michigan. Or compacts them in a car crusher. Or contracts out the hit. He hires the best shooters, pays top dollar."

"A man of respect?" Kaminski asked, quoting the old Mafia expression.

"You got it."

"What have *you* got, Harry? What are *you* offering me?"

Shannon looked around warily, saw that the pretty lieutenant was facing the other way and couldn't read his lips.

"What's the big secret, Harry?"

"Remember my son?"

"Blair, right? Nice boy. Last I heard he was with the Bureau in Denver."

"They moved him to Chicago fifteen months ago."

"How is he?" Kaminski asked.

Shannon stiffened before he answered.

"Dead."

The two men stared silently at the blank TV screen for a dozen seconds. Then Harry Shannon got up, took the cassette from the VCR, and called out to the black woman.

"Thank you, Lieutenant," he said.

She pressed the switch that opened the security door, and the two men left the chamber. Kaminski had no idea as to

what was in the other tapes in the large room designated
B-81, and he realized that he never would.

He didn't care.

He was much more concerned about two other questions.

Where was Shannon leading him now?

What was his plan?

11

The sound was deafening—and unmistakable.

Anyone who'd ever heard it before would recognize it immediately.

Kaminski knew it all too well, and it didn't rattle him.

This massive wall of noise was the sound of death and destruction—the brutal anthem of ground warfare.

When he and Ryan stepped out of the bunker, they were instantly assaulted by a tidal wave of blasts, whistles, and explosions. It crashed over them, and it didn't stop. This was the main firing range of Camp Lejeune, North Carolina, a place where determined young men were trained to become legends.

Every kind of infantry weapon in the Marine Corps' arsenal—and new hardware being tested—thundered around them. Howitzers and missiles, machine guns and mortars, grenade launchers and flamethrowers were all in action. The explosions of demolition charges and land mines hammered at the two civilians' ears like some murderous madrigal, and they felt the very earth beneath their feet tremble.

And there were self-propelled killing machines too. The cannon on a quartet of light tanks fired again and again. The armored vehicles' heavy machine guns swept back and forth, hammering like pneumatic drills.

Dante's *Inferno* in North Carolina, Kaminski thought.

This was organized hell.

Mark Kaminski knew about hell.

He'd been there. Two "tours" of savage combat in a distant Asian land had taught him a lot about hell.

Not everything but enough to survive.

No one ever knew it all. Thinking that you did led to mistakes—and funerals. Half of Kaminski's Special Forces team had come home in plastic sacks. Others were still in Veteran's Administration hospitals. Some of them didn't know anything—not even their own names.

Kaminski forced himself to push the memories back. He'd never get them out of his unconscious, but this wasn't the time to face them again. He had to concentrate on what Harry Shannon was saying.

They walked along side by side, trying to ignore the cataclysm around them. Shannon spoke low—under the thunder.

"I'll give it to you straight, Mark. I never liked the way you did things. You were the best FBI agent I knew, but you weren't a *good* one."

Kaminski shrugged.

"You broke every rule in the book—a dozen times," Shannon told him. "You ignored instructions, exceeded your authority, ran improper investigations . . . and, yes, used more force than regulations allowed. You made your own rules, and you operated like a goddam one-man army."

Shannon paused to light another cigarette.

"And those are the reasons I'm asking you to help me," he continued.

"How? What do you want?"

Shannon stopped and looked Kaminski squarely in the eyes.

"I want to destroy Luigi Patrovita."

"Why?"

"I owe it to my boy."

They started walking again, and Kaminski tried to make the connection between Ryan's dead son and The Emperor.

"You think he killed Blair?" Kaminski asked.

"And five other agents."

"That thing in the woods I read about?"

Shannon nodded.

"They were protecting a government witness who could have put Patrovita inside for life. Instead that bastard took theirs. It was his contract, Mark. He's gotta pay."

The older man had a strange look in his eye.

Probably shock at the murder of his firstborn. This was like the bible, Kaminski realized. An eye for an eye.

Did Shannon mean to enforce the Old Testament literally? Was he asking Mark Kaminski to kill?

"I'm a cop, not a hit man, Harry."

"I know that."

"And you've got to know there's nothing a country sheriff can do that you and the Bureau can't."

Shannon waited until another tank clattered past before he answered.

"You're wrong, Mark. I've got forty-five thousand dollars says you're wrong."

"Forty-five thousand?"

"My savings—every cent. If you need more, I'll sell the house. This is personal. I have to finance this thing myself."

Forty-five thousand dollars against Patrovita's guns and millions?

A bitter father's pride against the most powerful and vicious criminal organization in North America?

Only a fool or a romantic would even consider it.

"And what do I do with your forty-five, Harry?" he asked curiously.

"Get inside Patrovita's mob and rip it to pieces. You can do it—and I don't care how."

A flamethrower spat fire twenty yards away. The heat hit them like a fist.

"No one man is going to tear up the Patrovita organization," Kaminski said patiently. "Who do I look like, Clint Eastwood?"

"You look like a deeply unhappy man."

"And what the hell can you offer me to change that?" Kaminski erupted.

"Possible reinstatement. Back with the Bureau—doing what you do best."

It was preposterous—a vengeful father's desperate lie.

Still Kaminski had to ask the question.

"Exactly what have you got in mind?"

"We've been trying to get someone inside the Patrovita family for two and a half years. But there's a leak somewhere, and our guys keep getting blown away. One was burned alive. Two others just disappeared. That's why I've got to run this alone. I'm asking you to help, not commit suicide."

Shannon was clearly serious.

He really believed in this dangerous scheme.

"I'm the only one who'll know about you, Mark," he promised intensely. "I realize that it's a long shot, but it's not impossible."

"There are two possibilities—small and none."

"You want to rot the rest of your life in that tank town?" Shannon challenged. "Or do you want to take charge of your life? Pull this off and you'll have a good shot at being reinstated. It won't be just me hollering for you."

"Who else?"

"There'll be a hundred agents in the Chicago office—friends of the guys who got wasted in the woods—who'll march to D.C. and demand you get consideration. A hundred and one, including me. Don't you understand? You'll be a goddam hero!"

Kaminski weighed the odds.

"*Nobody* can keep out a hero," Shannon insisted.

Now Kaminski thought about his wife and her drift toward alcoholism.

Shannon's offer was impractical . . . almost irrational.

Still, it was the only one Mark Kaminski had.

"I do it *my* way?" he tested.

"You always did," Shannon replied with a grin as they shook hands.

"I won't even ask what you're doing," the graying FBI agent promised. "I *probably* wouldn't like the answers, anyway."

Then he realized that he was wrong.

There was no *question* about it.

It was a sure thing.

12

Step by step.

Kaminski knew that was the only way to do it.

And it had to be done exactly right—with no loose ends.

A single mistake could be disastrous. It would be worse than smoking cigarettes, he thought wryly as he drove toward the lights of Garrett six hours later. He recalled the warning printed on each pack that smoking is dangerous to your health. One error—any error—with the ruthless Patrovita mob would be *terminal*.

Not that Mark Kaminski smoked cigarettes.

That would be stupid for anyone who put in hours every day with the weights and other bodybuilding gear. Kaminski had always made a point of being in perfect condition. It wasn't just vanity or a way to attract women, though many females were fascinated by his superb physique. In the world that he'd chosen, total fitness was a way to stay alive.

It wasn't merely physical.

"A healthy mind in a healthy body," the Romans had said two thousand years earlier. He'd read a lot about the Romans, and he respected them. The fact that a tiny fraction of their descendants had degenerated into cunning criminals didn't affect that at all. He felt contempt for those who casually assumed that most Italian-Americans were Mafia hoodlums. The Mafia thugs were today's barbarians, the same breed that Rome had fought for centuries.

The Mafiosa was only some of today's barbarians—not all of them.

Organized crime was an equal opportunity employer—like law enforcement. Every cop knew that.

Kaminski also had quiet contempt for those who let their bodies and minds go flabby. They were decaying by the minute—both mentally and physically—because they were lazy. They had no discipline. Discipline was important to Mark Kaminski. He believed in controlling his own life in both quality and quantity.

That was why he was taking on this dangerous job.

Just as he planned his exercises, he planned his attack. Physical strength wouldn't be enough. His brain was as much a weapon as his powerful body. He had to outsmart The Emperor.

Step by step.

And the first step was going to be unpleasant. Kaminski was an honest man. That was his nature, and it had often gotten him into trouble. Even small evasions did not come easily to him. Lying was harder. Now he had to do something he'd never done before—lie to the woman he loved.

To protect her.

To save his own life.

He knew that there was no alternative, but he didn't like it.

He'd always thought that lying was for the weak. Now he had to find the strength to do it himself.

She had already suffered so much, and this was going to bring her a new and terrible pain. It might last for months.

But if the risky plan worked, they would both lead better lives. It had to work. He'd make it.

When he entered his house, he embraced and kissed her—and lied.

"Sorry I'm late," he said, "but I've got some good news for a change. We may be leaving here."

"Are you serious?"

"Dead serious," he answered, with no intention to make a clever play on words. "I drove over to Raleigh to talk to an old friend who phoned this morning. He's just been named assistant chief of police in Philadelphia, and he thinks he can hire me."

"Oh, my God!"

"The pay would be double what I get here, and Philadelphia's got all those things you miss."

Her whole face lit up in anticipation.

She looked at the half-empty bottle of beer in her hand, walked to the sink, and poured the remaining contents down the drain.

"Don't need it," she said joyously. "We'll be drinking wine again in Philadelphia. When do we go?"

"It might take eight or ten weeks. He's got to arrange the paperwork."

"But it's definite?"

"About ninety-five percent. Yeah, I'd say you can start packing soon."

She hugged him again.

"I'll start tomorrow."

"Not tonight?" he said, joking.

"I've got other plans for tonight, Mr. Kaminski," she announced with a mischievous grin, and nodded toward the bedroom.

She radiated happiness.

Amy Kaminski had no suspicion that she'd be weeping a widow's tears in less than forty-eight hours.

13

It was a lousy night to die.

A fine full moon soothed the North Carolina country-side with silvery rays, and the temperature was a pleasant fifty-nine degrees. There was hardly a cloud in the sky.

Kaminski didn't *want* to die tonight.

It would be better to wait for a darker evening dressed in shadows that reduced visibility, he thought as he drove the police cruiser down the two-lane road a mile outside the Barrett town line. The blackness would reduce the chance of being seen.

Darkness did not trouble him. He was used to it. In Nam he'd been one of the best night fighters. He had superb night vision—as many enemy soldiers had learned the hard way. The hardest way of all.

He had excellent hearing too. He had the extraordinary ears of an animal, moving surely and silently through the jungle like some man-tiger. Chicago would only be another kind of jungle, he thought. The tall buildings, crowded streets, and heavy traffic wouldn't make that much of a difference. As in Nam, death would never be more than ten yards away.

His survival would still depend on his reflexes and cunning. But in Chicago *he* would be the guerrilla infiltrator seeking invisibility. In that dense forest of concrete and steel towers he would be the Cong—blending into the urban landscape. The numerous and well-entrenched Patrovita mob had the firepower. They held the High Ground.

He'd be in constant danger.

There would be no reinforcements or allies whom he could turn to—nobody he could trust. The informer who had sold out the FBI team in the safe house probably wasn't the only one. With huge funds and years to find corrupt collaborators, The Emperor probably had a score of greedy spies in the law-enforcement community.

That situation wasn't unique to Chicago, of course.

There were always a few crooked cops and other civil servants everywhere. Today that included federal people too.

When Kaminski had joined the Bureau, it had been unthinkable that an FBI agent could go bad. In recent years American society had changed—for the worse. Every month brought fresh headlines about citizens of this great and free democracy who connived with foreign powers, dope dealers, and other criminals.

And every month more people were less surprised.

Though he was disgusted by the growing nonchalance about the "me and money" vermin, Kaminski was much too realistic to ignore them. The infection could not be denied. One more reason for taking this risky assignment was that he could identify and expose the "respectable" public employees who had betrayed the agents gunned down at the safe house and the three undercover operatives.

Unless he did, they'd sell out more.

He could be the next victim himself, but that wasn't the only reason. Kaminski was honest enough to admit that he felt a powerful urge to get even. It was more than a desire. It was a need. Though the Bureau had let him down, he was not free of it. He still cared enough about the FBI to hate the men who'd murdered the nine agents. The killers had to pay, and so did those who had paid them.

It was the traditional cop's code—still alive in police departments everywhere. Kaminski was old-fashioned enough to respect it, for in respecting that law he respected himself. He was still a cop. He always would be.

He looked at his watch.

It was time to get ready to die.

He lifted the radiophone on the dashboard.

"Kaminski to base. Kaminski to base. I'm out on Route Twelve, checking out lights at the old Petrochem Storage Depot. May be a prowler inside. Out."

He saw the nine-foot-high wire fence a minute later. It ringed a small oil and gasoline storage complex put up by Petrochem Inc., which had gone belly-up in bankruptcy two years earlier.

The depot wasn't anything fancy.

Four smallish storage tanks—each thirty-one feet high, linked to each other by umbilical connections of pipes, cables, ducts and wiring. There was a pumping unit at the north end. What wasn't stained with rust needed paint. It wasn't a fuel operation anymore. It was a graveyard for a dead dream.

The sign on the chain-link gate said it all.

PLANT CLOSED . . . NO TRESPASSING . . . DANGER

Kaminski stopped near the gate, turned off the police car's lights, and walked across the road. He pushed aside the underbrush, advanced ten yards, and found the camouflage tarp that he'd covered with branches the previous night. He shoved the branches aside and pulled away the cloth.

There it was.

His way out.

The motorcycle was smaller than the powerful highway patrol model that the fake cop had driven, but it would do the job. He brought it to the entrance of the depot, took bolt cutters from the trunk of his cruiser, and severed the lock on the gate.

Then he swung it open and drove the car inside. He had to move quickly. That was no problem. He'd reconnoitered the target as carefully as if it were a Viet Cong ammo dump, and he knew precisely what he had to do.

He parked the car beside one of the abandoned storage tanks, got out, and studied the pipes. The bright moonlight helped him find what he needed—a valve. He reached to twist it open.

It didn't move.

It was stuck—hard. The thing hadn't been turned in twenty-four months. Grit and rust owned it now.

He had to open the valve. The plan depended on it. There was no time to spare. Somebody might drive by at any moment . . . might see the cruiser.

He took a lug wrench from the cruiser's trunk. First he slammed it against the valve three . . . four . . . five times. Then he slid the wrench handle into the valve spokes and applied pressure.

It didn't budge.

But Kaminski wouldn't yield, either. Using the strength of his powerful arms, bracing his superbly conditioned body, and concentrating his will, he tried again. Sweat streamed and his muscles bulged. The seconds ticked away relentlessly.

It was man against metal.

This man won.

The valve moved—a quarter of an inch.

He applied more pressure and the metal surrendered.

The valve reluctantly yielded, stuck again, and finally rotated fully. A stream of gasoline spilled from the tank, forming a small puddle near his feet. It stopped, and Kaminski shook his head grimly.

He needed a lot more than this. He hit the valve with the wrench again, and the flow resumed. It had probably been some sludge or perhaps an air bubble that had clogged the outlet, he thought as the pool of petroleum widened steadily.

So far, so good—but he had to hurry.

He walked to the motorcycle parked outside the fence, climbed on, and drove a hundred yards to a rise in the road. He opened a plastic container bolted to the cycle, took out a short-barreled Stoner carbine, and peered back at his car. He aimed carefully.

He had to hit the vehicle's gas tank with the first shot. It could threaten his entire plan if they found several bullet holes in the wreckage. Kaminski, who'd qualified as a sharpshooter, squeezed the trigger slowly.

Bull's-eye.

The explosive round struck its mark. The cruiser erupted into flames. After a few seconds the fire reached the smelly pool of stagnant gasoline. The blast came only a moment later. The storage tank exploded like a thousand-pound bomb, sending shock waves out like massive fists and spraying a rain of burning droplets over the other tanks.

More explosions.

More fires.

More devastation to melt the cruiser and incinerate everything in it that wasn't metal.

He'd left his police pistol, belt, wristwatch, car and house keys, and a favorite Swiss Army knife on the front seat with his sheriff's badge. Just in case the fire didn't quite consume everything, he'd put his wallet and a pair of his boots on the floor nearby.

The whole Petrochem Depot was ablaze, spouting flames eighty feet into the October night. Kaminski looked at the raging conflagration for several seconds before he put the carbine back in the plastic box and got on the motorcycle.

He started the engine, rode fifty yards to the crest, and glanced back again. He couldn't even see the cruiser anymore. There was a ball of fire where it had been. The police car was gone.

So was Sheriff Mark Kaminski.

There wouldn't be any meticulous scientific analysis of the ashes—not in this small rural town. Nobody would call in the FBI's masterful laboratory teams to study this debris with ultradelicate equipment.

The local paper would report the unfortunate industrial accident, and a minister or two would say kind words about the deceased next Sunday. After giving the widow his condolences and the proceeds of the sheriff's ten-thousand-dollar life insurance policy, the mayor would find a replacement to head the town's little police department.

By that time the man on the motorcycle would be far away. No one would be looking for him. They'd all think he was dead.

He'd have a new name . . . new clothes . . . new gun.

He'd need the weapon to stay alive where he was going.

Chicago.

14

Northwest.
    Five miles an hour below the speed limit.

He drove the cycle through the Carolina night for three hours before he pulled to the side of the road. He retrieved the five-gallon can he'd hidden the previous evening and refilled the motorbike's tank. This way there'd be no risk that some gas station attendant might recognize his face from a newspaper photo of the "sheriff who died in the fire."

Keeping off the main roads, he rode on across the state line into Virginia. Even there he wasn't safe. He pushed on for another ninety minutes until he came to a bridge over a river some eighty yards wide. He drove out to the middle, took the carbine from the plastic cargo box, and carefully wiped any fingerprints from the weapon.

He listened, looked in both directions, and saw no lights from houses or vehicles. The water should be deepest here. He threw the carbine in a high arc and saw it sink. Then he resumed his journey.

Northwest toward West Virginia. He got there in midmorning. He was alert, but his eyes were tired. He stopped to drink coffee from the thermos he'd stored in the cargo box. That stimulant would help—for a while. A while was all he needed.

At eleven o'clock he saw that his tank was nearly empty. He was beginning to feel the fatigue. A roadside sign announced that Red's Gas was a mile and a half ahead. He squinted as he read it. The glare of the morning sun was bothering his weary eyes. Kaminski sighed and rode on.

Red's was a two-pump operation. When Kaminski dismounted, he saw a balding man—maybe sixty and surely forty pounds overweight—inside the station. Kaminski waved at him, and he gestured back casually for Kaminski to put in the gas himself. Then the fat man returned his attention to the copy of last May's *Playboy* in his lap.

The sun was very bright. Kaminski inserted the nozzle into the cycle's tank, sighed, and looked around automatically. He saw that Red's was on the edge of a little community a tenth the size of Barrett.

Amy ought to try *this* town on, he thought as he took a pair of Foster Grant aviator sunglasses from his jacket and put them on. A greasy-haired young drifter watched him furtively from behind a nearby clump of trees.

When the tank was full, Kaminski went inside to pay.

"Just over four gallons," he said and put down a ten-dollar bill.

The big-bellied man took another look at Miss May's jutting young mammaries, grunted, and handed Kaminski his change.

"You ever see jugs like that?" he asked.

Kaminski nodded truthfully.

"You're lucky. Those got to be thirty-eight C's. *At least* thirty-eight C's," the older man declared. He held up the centerfold.

Thirty-six B, Kaminski computed silently, but why spoil the older man's fantasy?

"Toilet?" Kaminski asked.

"Around back. Jeezus—thirty-eight C! That's something!"

As Kaminski emerged from the primitive lavatory he heard a sound that he recognized immediately. He stepped out into the glare to see the greasy-haired stranger—maybe twenty-two or twenty-three—on his cycle. The son of a bitch was trying to steal it.

In a split second the fatigue was gone.

The thief gunned the engine. Kaminski was already running. As the cycle began to pick up speed Kaminski reached the rack stacked with cans of motor oil. He grabbed one as the motorcycle tore past him.

Kaminski hurled the can with all his might.

It flew straight and true.

The can caught the thief squarely in the back of the skull and knocked him flying from the motorcycle. As his face met the side of a battered '75 Ford pickup parked near the road, Kaminski charged toward him. Uncontrolled, the bike bounced over a rock and tumbled into a ditch.

The thief was unconscious when Kaminski reached him. Blood seeped from his clearly broken nose, and more carmine dripped from his mouth. His jaw was askew. It would take a good dentist to fix that, Kaminski estimated.

And the oilcan was badly dented from the impact. Mark Kaminski picked it up and studied it. Then he carried it inside the gas station.

"And a quart of oil," Kaminski said coolly.

Without saying a word the porky *Playboy* enthusiast

charged him eighty cents more than the going price for this brand. It figured.

"I think you'd better call an ambulance for *him*," Kaminski said as he pocketed the change.

"Why don't you take him with you?"

Kaminski shook his head.

"*Shit*," the older man grumbled.

"So long, Red."

"Red's been dead for nine years."

Kaminski shrugged and walked to his cycle. He raised it, climbed on, and hit the starter. The motor coughed, sputtered, and came to life. Kaminski put the can of oil in the plastic cargo box, closed it securely, and glanced back.

The man who wasn't Red was still ogling Miss May's ample body as Kaminski stepped on the gas pedal and drove away.

15

*H*e had to get rid of the motorcycle.

When he reached Parkersburg on the Ohio line, he did.

It was easy.

He drove it into a shabby part of the city, parked it in an alley behind a sleazy-looking strip joint, and removed the North Carolina plates. Then he headed for the bus terminal, confident that somebody would steal the machine within a few hours.

He reached the motel in Indianapolis the next afternoon. The package that Harry Shannon had express-mailed was waiting for him when he registered under the prearranged name. He took it to his room with his shoulder bag, locked the door, and drew the curtains. Then he put both items on the bed.

He extracted from the bag the bottle of hair dye that he'd bought downtown near the bus station and went to work. He applied the color carefully, following the instructions step by step. He needed a new appearance for his new identity.

Changing his hair from brown to a dark black was a key part of the alteration.

When he was nearly done, he opened Shannon's package. He removed the contents and set each item down on top of the dresser.

One 38-caliber Beretta automatic pistol.

One well-worn shoulder holster.

Two boxes of ammunition.

A switchblade—right for his new identity as hood.

Three bulging envelopes and a miniature tape recorder.

He turned on the recorder and resumed touching up his hair.

"Welcome to Indianapolis," Shannon's voice greeted. "I'm sorry you had to kill off Mark Kaminski, but it had to be done. If you run into someone who thinks he recognizes you, it could protect you—and your wife. Those animals would rip her to pieces."

Kaminski nodded, applied more dye.

"Think of it this way, Mark. With any luck you'll be home with her before she's out of mourning."

Kaminski frowned.

He knew that a man made his own luck.

He began experimenting with different ways to comb his new hair—ways that would significantly change his appearance.

"One envelope has your new ID papers, Mr. Brenner. Joseph C. Brenner, a real bad guy. You've got quite a record, Joey. The NCIC computer in Washington has an impressive rap sheet for Joey Brenner—with your fingerprints."

Kaminski used the comb to try another hairstyle.

"These pricks are going to check you out, Joey. They run a big-league operation—very modern. We know they've got crooked cops on the payroll, and one of those roaches can tap into the FBI computer in sixty seconds flat. You've got to come up goon—or you go down in the lake with the fish.''

Like the other undercover agents who'd preceded him.

"You'll find twenty-five thousand for initial expenses. You're not just a punk kid. You're a successful gun—a somebody. A somebody doesn't show in Chicago without walking around money. You've got to have a roll for the Patrovita mob to take you seriously. Now look in the big envelope.''

Kaminski complied. He took out several eight-by-ten black-and-white photographs and a slip of paper. Several numerals were written on it.

"That phone number is your only way to communicate with me. If you have important news or *really* need help, call. Anytime, day or night. It'll get you an answering machine in a safe house I've rented in west Chicago. I'll check the machine by remote control—I've got a beeper— every couple of hours. If you're in trouble, I'll come running.''

Probably not in time.

Trouble meant he'd been spotted.

If he were identified as a cop, he'd be dead in three minutes—unless The Emperor chose to prolong the agony.

"Now take a look at the pictures, Joey.''

Patrovita, Rocca—The Undertaker—and a third face he'd never seen.

Beetle brows . . . curly hair . . . mean, greedy eyes.

There was nasty ambition and cruelty in that face.

"The third ape is just as vicious as the other two. His name is Ben Lamansky. Very tricky—they call him The Snake. The Snake Lamansky used to work for Patrovita. Now he's got his own mob, and he's cutting in on The Emperor's pie.''

Studying his appearance in the mirror, Kaminski decided

that Joey Brenner needed a whole new wardrobe! Flashy clothes, the ostentatiously expensive and vulgar attire of a successful triggerman. He'd buy them in the morning . . . wear them for a few days before he reached Chicago.

Fat silk ties.

Boldly colored shirts.

Sharp shoes—essential for hoodlum chic.

A gold chain or bracelet wouldn't hurt, either.

"Patrovita hates this Lamansky," Shannon continued. "One way you might catch Patrovita's eye would be to make trouble for The Snake's operation. The Emperor might appreciate that."

But Ben Lamansky wouldn't.

Even if Patrovita's gang accepted Joey Brenner, Lamansky's gunmen would be out to blast him.

Kaminski glanced at the photo of The Snake, scowled, and gave him an obscene single-finger salute—as Joey Brenner would. Kaminski had to get into the part immediately and play it to the hilt.

Or die.

He might do that, anyway.

"Lamansky's got a lot of gambling joints, cathouses, and other businesses. There's a list of most of them—with addresses. He's got armed muscle at every one of them, and you can assume that he's bought some cops too."

Great.

The odds were getting worse by the second.

"So be careful. Don't trust anybody. I'm counting on you . . . and so is my son. You can do it, kid. Give 'em hell!"

Silence. The briefing was over.

He strapped on the shoulder holster. Then he loaded the automatic and slid it into the sheath under his left armpit. After he placed the shoulder bag and the contents of

Shannon's package in a drawer, he put on his jacket and glanced at his wrist.

There was no watch.

He'd left it behind in the cruiser. It was melted junk now.

He reached into the drawer, found the envelope with the cash, and slid it into the inside breast pocket of the jacket.

Even without the watch he knew what time it was.

It was time to buy some flashy clothes and an ostentatious new timepiece.

It was time for the hoodlum killer named Joey Brenner to go to work.

16

There were seven men in the huge warehouse.

Four at one end . . . three at the other.

Every one of them was armed.

All had killed before and were ready to do it again.

Now.

The quartet advanced slowly down the wide aisle, walking and looking as if they might be entering a mine field.

Luigi Patrovita . . . Paul Rocca . . . Tony Milan . . . Eddie Shea.

Rocca strode half a step behind The Emperor—a sign of respect. Wide-shouldered Tony Milan and wiry Eddie Shea trailed three yards behind. They were Patrovita's personal bodyguards. Their overcoats were unbuttoned and their hands were half raised—ready to draw their guns at a second's notice.

Their eyes roved back and forth . . . up and down. Even though Patrovita had chosen this place, they weren't comfortable. Most of the warehouse was in shadows. Only this aisle between the pallets stacked with crates was illuminated by a row of overhead lights.

The three men at the other end of the aisle had their coats unbuttoned too. Ben Lamansky and his two bodyguards weren't taking any chances. They watched tensely as the four approached.

Patrovita stopped ten feet from Lamansky and glared.

Ben Lamansky smiled to show he wasn't afraid.

Then he ostentatiously looked at his platinum wristwatch.

"Hope this won't take long," he said. "Costs me a bundle when we get together like this. Now my time's worth as much as yours," he boasted.

"It's worth more," Rocca announced venomously, " 'cause you got less of it."

"I don't talk to the help," Lamansky replied.

Aware of Rocca's temper, The Emperor gestured for his enforcer to control his fury.

"I'll talk," Patrovita said slowly. "I called this meet to do you a favor, Ben."

"Don't need any favors, Luigi."

"You used to be a good guy," Patrovita continued as he ignored the presumptuous provocation. "I'm giving you the courtesy of talking because you worked for me for a long time. I'll make it short. Close down and get out."

Lamansky lit a cigarette and blew a perfect smoke ring.

"Can't do that, Luigi," he replied. "I've got a lot of employees—and obligations. Customers who depend on me. Wouldn't be right to let them all down."

"It's over—period."

"Come on, old buddy, there's plenty for both of us."

"There's no *both of us*, Ben. There's just *me*," Patrovita said bluntly. "You got plenty of money and two days to shut down. Take three if you have to—seventy-two hours."

Lamansky blew another smoke ring.

"Then what?" he asked. "Back to work for you?"

"Not for me or anyone else in Chicago. Try Hawaii, Ben. They say the swimming's good. The water's warmer than Lake Michigan."

The threat was clear.

Quit or die.

Patrovita didn't wait for Lamansky to answer. The Emperor had spoken. He turned on his heel and started for the exit. Rocca followed, with the bodyguards backing out behind him.

The meeting was over.

17

Half past two the next afternoon.

Chicago's near North Side beside the lake—a high-rent area where many of the city's best restaurants are located.

Satisfied diners and affluent local residents were strolling the pleasant streets in a steady stream, enjoying that simple sense of well being that comes from a fine meal and a plump bank account. There were no scruffy panhandlers or foul-breathed winos to offend the American Express Card crowd here. Conscientious police—who did very well at Christmas—kept them away.

Even the vehicles parked along these fashionable curbs were upscale. Mercedes, BMWs, Caddys, Lincolns, Jags, Porsches, and Maseratis dozed in splendor beside freshly waxed Rolls and Lamborghinis. The old school bus that squatted on a side street was definitely out of place, but it had a new coat of white paint and lettering identifying it as property of the Chicago Boys Club—a worthy charity. Charity was always "in," so nobody minded.

Half a block south of the corner where the bus sat was the Szechuan Gourmet, an excellent Chinese restaurant. Even though Windy City sophisticates knew that Szechuan was last year's Chinese cuisine, some still patronized the Szechuan Gourmet for its very good service and witty fortune cookies. Others—less refined—came for the spicy food and big drinks.

Luigi Patrovita was in the second group. At 2:32 P.M., two of his men came out of the Chinese restaurant, scanned the street in both directions, and opened the Szechuan Gourmet's door again.

They nodded.

Bodyguard Tony Milan exited next, and Patrovita and Rocca followed. Mellow with the effects of twenty-year-old Ambassador Scotch, they joked as they started toward the bulletproof stretch limousine that waited for them twenty yards away. Rocca waved at the chauffeur, who immediately started the black Cadillac's engine.

The bus turned the corner and headed toward them. They didn't notice that the windows were oddly obscured by dark stain or paint. They didn't pay any attention to the old vehicle as it lumbered nearer.

As Patrovita and his full-bellied employees reached The Emperor's long limousine, Rocca belched and Patrovita took a four-dollar Havana corona from his leather cigar case. Bodyguard Milan immediately produced a lighter.

He didn't flick it, though. Three of the windows on the street side of the bus rose a few inches. The muzzles of submachine guns blossomed at each opening, and the automatic weapons blasted in deadly chorus.

Bullets ripped the front of the building and dropped the limousine chauffeur. Tony Milan reacted instantly—without thinking. He did what he'd been paid a thousand dollars a week to do. He stepped between Luigi Patrovita and the machine guns, pushing his stunned employer to the sidewalk.

He was on the pavement beside Patrovita a moment later, but he didn't know it. He wasn't a bodyguard anymore, just a statistic. Five bullets had made the conversion. The FBI didn't have to worry about him now. His future lay with the Cook County coroner.

People were screaming and dodging behind cars. Others dived to the cement, astounded that this could happen in a good neighborhood *today*. Rocca and the two surviving bodyguards were firing at the bus as fast as they could.

It wasn't fast enough.

Tires screeching as rubber burned, the bus careened around the next corner and disappeared. Though he couldn't see it, Paul Rocca knew where the white ambush vehicle was going. It would race eight or ten blocks, turn up an alley where two cars were waiting, engines running. The hit team would split up and drive off in opposite directions at legal speed.

He'd done it that way himself—three times.

Years ago, before he became an executive who put out contracts instead of doing the killing himself.

All this flashed through his mind in an instant. Then he turned his attention to Patrovita on the sidewalk beside him.

"Luigi, you okay?" he asked hoarsely.

With the bloody remains of Tony Milan sprawled across his legs, The Emperor of the Midwest underworld cursed and nodded. Then he cursed again.

"Fuck you, Lamansky! I'm alive! Not a scratch! I'll get you for this, you son of a bitch! You're dog meat!"

He glared down at the body, shook his head, and pushed the corpse off his legs angrily. There were bloodstains all over his jacket and trousers. An eight-hundred-dollar tailor-made suit—ruined!

Rocca leaned over to examine the body.

"He's gone."

"Shit," Patrovita swore as he struggled to his feet shakily. "We're dealing with a lunatic. That goddamn Lamansky's *crazy*. How could he think he could take me out just like that? *Me*?"

The lunatic nearly got you, Rocca thought, but he didn't say it. That wouldn't be wise with The Emperor in such a rage.

"Cops'll be along any minute," he warned. "Let's get out of here."

The other bodyguards picked up the corpse. They followed Rocca as he guided the unsteady Patrovita to the limousine. They saw that the chauffeur was bleeding but still conscious.

"How bad is it, Eddie?" Rocca asked.

"I'll make it—but you better drive," Shea answered.

Patrovita leaned on Rocca as the bodyguards manhandled Milan's body into the backseat. They hurried in beside it as a distant police siren sounded.

"Tony was a good boy," The Emperor said in grim approval.

Rocca opened the front door near the curb, helped Patrovita in.

"*Real* good," Luigi Patrovita continued. "Now you go get me someone just as good."

"Sure," Rocca promised.

He climbed in, pushed Shea over, and slid behind the wheel. The armored limousine was five blocks away when the police cars arrived. Guns drawn, four uniformed cops jumped out and asked white-faced people cowering in the doorways what had happened.

Nobody could remember.

18

There was nothing fancy about the big room.

This place wasn't for the high rollers.

It was a standard backroom gambling setup in a working-class neighborhood.

Three poker tables, two crap tables, a couple of betting windows, and a king-and-a-half-sized projection television screen displaying the horse races in progress at Aqueduct. A round-faced man with the cauliflower ear of an ex-boxer was pouring cheap rye at a small bar.

At one of the crap tables Joey C. Brenner stood in his flashy new clothes. He blew on his cupped palm and threw the dice.

"Seven—you lose. Try again, Jack," the stickman invited.

"What for? I don't think the table's straight," Brenner said.

"Losers never do," the stickman jeered

Brenner pulled two ball bearings from his jacket pocket, rolled them down the table. The magnets concealed underneath made them veer in dramatically erratic routes.

"Sometimes losers are right," Brenner said. "I want to see Lamansky. Now."

"He left, Jack. Why don't you?"

"I got a better idea."

Brenner wrapped his powerful arms around the table, lifted the heavy piece of furniture, and heaved it over onto its side. First there was a crash of splintering wood. Then people began to shout as chaos swept the casino.

"Rudy! Rudy!" the stickman bellowed urgently.

A large man—about six-foot-three and two hundred and fifty pounds—came charging across the room. So did two other beefy types. The customers panicked and started to flee as the three bouncers converged on Joey C. Brenner.

It would take them about four seconds to arrive, he computed.

First things first.

He pulled back his right fist, rifled a hard punch to the arrogant stickman's jaw, and saw the crook reel back and crack his head against the wall.

Feeling better, Brenner turned his attention to the bouncers. He slammed a karate chop to the first one's neck, then punched him in the solar plexus. The goon fell over a poker table, gasping for breath.

Brenner spun on his heel as the big man arrived growling. He stopped growling and made another sound when Brenner kicked him in the stomach. He doubled up like an accordion. An uppercut straightened him for a second before Brenner grabbed him by one arm, swung him in a circle, and rammed him into the wooden bar.

With his forehead split open and five teeth shattered, the big man whimpered through bleeding lips as he slid to the floor. The bartender grabbed an eighteen-inch club, its end wrapped in steel chain. He smiled triumphantly as he leaned across the bar to smash the troublemaker.

Brenner dodged the blow easily. Moving with startling speed, he jerked the club from the startled bartender's grasp. An instant later Brenner reversed it like a drum major's baton and expertly broke his attacker's right wrist.

The bartender howled, tried to hit Brenner with a beer bottle. Now Brenner dragged him over the bar, picked him up as if he were a Barbie doll, and threw him through the closed window into the rear alley.

The third bouncer furtively approached Brenner from behind. He popped open a six-inch switchblade and raised it to stab Brenner in the back. Catching a glimpse of him in the mirror behind the bar, Brenner kicked back like the black belt he was. The would-be killer dropped the switchblade to clutch his agonized groin.

He fell to his knees, making unintelligible noises that sounded animal. They grew less audible when Brenner put a metal wastebasket over his head and banged on it twice with the club.

The gamblers were fleeing in desperation. Frantic men and women ran out through the restaurant that was the front for the casino—frightening diners with their screams. In the rear gambling area the muscular man who called himself Joey C. Brenner prepared to hurt Lamansky where it really counted.

His pocketbook.

Personnel could be replaced. Property was more costly.

He set to work methodically. He shattered the mirror that had saved his life, and then smashed the bar itself. Eight swift blows with the metal-tipped club reduced it to scrap lumber. At that point Rudy lurched to his feet and came at him with a chair. Brenner stepped aside, twisted it from his hand, and broke it over his head.

Then Brenner resumed the demolition job. He lifted one poker table over his head, used it as a hammer to bust up another. He threw the third one over the bar, shattering half a dozen bottles and spraying liquor in a wide arc. After that he vaulted the bar like an Olympic gymnast. There was nothing sportsmanlike about the way he broke every glass. It was dull work, but someone had to do it.

When he turned, he saw another bouncer reaching for a snub-barreled belly gun on the floor. Brenner jumped the bar again, tapped the weapon away with the club, and pulled the groggy hoodlum to his feet.

"Guns I don't like," Brenner said and poleaxed him with a punch squarely between the eyes. The thug fell to the floor, flopping like a fish out of water.

Now Brenner scanned the wreckage, material and human.

"This joint's a mess," he told the battered quartet. "Better clean it up before Lamansky gets back."

He started for the door. As it closed behind him, Rudy noticed the gun and began crawling toward it.

Brenner made his way through the restaurant, brushing splinters of wood and glass from his clothes as diners gaped. As he walked out to the street he noticed the Automobile Club tow truck on the far side. He strode across quickly.

"I'd like to borrow your rig for a minute," he told the startled driver. "It's okay. I'm a paid-up member. Here's my card."

He raised the vicious-looking club, and the driver fled.

Brenner started the truck, saw vehicles coming from both directions, and decided that he couldn't wait. He cut across traffic, aiming the truck at the front of the restaurant. A dozen fascinated pedestrians stood near the door, watching and wondering.

Brenner stopped the truck and stuck his head out the window. These people were in his way.

"Excuse me," he said politely. "Would you please move over about ten yards? Thanks."

They stepped aside, visibly puzzled.

"I've got a delivery to make," he explained.

Then he gunned the motor and crashed the truck through the front of the building—into the restaurant.

Then right on through it as hysterical diners leapt aside.

At that moment Rudy and the other three hoodlums entered the rear of the restaurant from the ravaged gambling joint behind it. Rudy had the gun in his belt and a hunger for revenge burning in his large belly. He was determined to kill the stranger who'd ruined his dignity and the casino.

He changed his mind when he saw the truck coming at him at thirty miles an hour. He turned and ran. So did his terrified companions. The truck barreled on, sending tables and chairs and potted plants flying as it bulldozed a patch through the dining room.

Here was the wall that hid the gambling club.

Not for long.

Brenner rammed the truck through it, ripping apart pipes and raping wiring systems as he broke through. Water spouted. Steam gushed. Shorted electrical connections crackled and sputtered menacingly. The casino looked as if it had been hit by a bomb.

There was debris everywhere.

Some of it was heaped on two of the bouncers. A heavy dice table pinned the bartender to the floor. The big man was on his knees, groping for his gun.

He decided not to continue when Brenner drove the truck to within an inch of his face. Frozen with fear, all he could do was stare at the heavy machine—so near. He could feel the heat of the motor. It was still running. If the man behind the wheel slid the gear from neutral, Rudy would be pulped.

Brenner climbed down, waked around, and sent the pistol flying with a precisely aimed kick.

"I *said* no guns," he reminded.

He reeled off ten yards of steel cable from the truck's winch, secured the hook around the room's main pillar, which supported the ceiling, and got back behind the wheel.

"Have a good day, fellas," he said cheerfully as he released the clutch. The truck moved forward. As it smashed its own door out the back wall of the building, the cable tightened and pulled out the supporting beam. Something creaked and swayed overhead.

Then the entire roof of the casino collapsed.

19

Patrovita's "main" car was gangland's standard status symbol—a big black Cadillac.

Ben Lamansky's regular vehicle was an even larger Caddy—four feet longer and painted dark maroon.

At three P.M. on the day after loyal Tony Milan died, Lamansky's lavishly appointed limousine was parked outside Chicago's most expensive jewelry store. The mustachioed twenty-nine-year-old man lounging behind the wheel knew a lot about cars. He'd stolen nearly five hundred of them before becoming Lamansky's driver.

Despite the sense of security that came with a regular weekly check, he sometimes missed the excitement of his previous work. Driving the maroon limo was often boring, and the waiting around was even worse. That was why he yawned as he read the racing pages of the afternoon paper.

He wondered how long she could shop.

How much damn jewelry could the voluptuous blonde buy?

She had to be dynamite in bed, the chauffeur thought.

Why else would a smart guy like Lamansky give her all these charge accounts?

The driver started to yawn again. He stopped when Joey Brenner suddenly appeared from nowhere, opened the rear door, and slid in behind him.

"You got the wrong car, pal."

"But the right piece," Brenner replied, showing the Beretta automatic.

"You know who owns these wheels?"

"A jerk who'll probably be buried before it's out of warranty," Brenner taunted. "Now be quiet, stupid."

He put the muzzle of the .38 against the driver's head. Impressed by this lethal logic, the man behind the wheel stopped talking. He began to perspire. Even if the lunatic with the Beretta didn't blast him, he'd still have to face Lamansky's wrath.

He was covered with sweat half a minute later when the rear door on the curb side opened. An eye-catching blonde— twenty-four years old and built like a young Marilyn Monroe— leaned down to enter.

She was surprised to see a stranger.

Then she was frightened when he waved the gun toward her.

"What are you doing?" she blurted.

Brenner reached out, grabbed her wrist and a handful of her expensive silk dress, and yanked her into the limousine.

"Waiting for you, Gloria," he announced.

Then he shoved the Beretta muzzle against the chauffeur's head again.

"Let's take a drive, Al—south."

This wasn't any ordinary junkie car thief, the man behind the wheel thought as he obeyed. The bastard knew his name and Gloria's too. Who the hell was he?

Not one of Patrovita's mob.

The Emperor would have sent a squad.

Whoever he was, he knew exactly where he was going and gave specific driving instructions. Some twenty minutes later he ordered the perspiration-drenched chauffeur to stop near a large group of institutional-looking buildings.

"The jewelry—all of it," he told the buxom blonde.

"You know who paid for these rocks?" she asked shrilly.

"A creep named Lamansky. You're making a mistake, Gloria. Nice girl like you shouldn't sleep with a snake."

He held out his hand.

"The rocks, Gloria."

She hesitated until he raised a massive fist.

"You got a beautiful face," he said flatly.

The threat was clear. She immediately took off and gave him every piece. It was worth $120,000, but her face was worth more. It was a big part of her working capital, and she wasn't about to blow it. She could play Lamansky's ego and body like a harmonica. He'd buy her new jewelry.

"Now peel off your clothes," the man with the gun ordered.

"*Me?*" she squealed.

"Both of you."

"*Everything?*" she protested.

"Keep the underwear. Wouldn't want you to catch a cold."

After they complied, he told them to get out of the car. As they left the Cadillac a group of young people in their late teens stopped to star at the mustachioed man in T-shirt and Jockey shorts and the pretty blonde overflowing her lacy brassiere and lavender bikini panties.

"*Now* what do we do?" she asked indignantly.

"This is the University of Chicago. Take a course," he advised as he tossed her purse to her. Then he took a twenty-dollar bill from his pocket and handed it to the gangster's mistress.

"Cab fare," he explained.

First he scared her . . . then he ripped off all her jewelry . . . and next he made her strip half naked. It didn't make sense for him to give her twenty dollars of his own money to get home. She looked at him again. He was actually handsome. Yeah, *very* handsome.

"What's your name?" she wondered aloud.

"Joey," he replied, and drove off at once. The neighborhood a mile away where he stopped at a grocery was like a Park Avenue "society" woman's cocktail dress—basic black. He made two purchases in the store.

A pound of white sugar.

A large plastic jug of bleach.

When he reached a low-traffic area of small houses, he put the sugar in the Cadillac's engine and splashed the powerful bleach all over the upholstery.

Lamansky would get the message, and the story of his humiliation would spread through the underworld.

Luigi Patrovita would hear about it.

He did—the next morning.

20

The hotel had sixteen floors, suites that rented for as much as $550 a night, and a uniformed doorman who spoke with an appealing Irish brogue. The wood-paneled lobby was immaculate and decorated in the old-fashioned way, with large potted plants, not hookers.

It was obviously one of Chicago's finer hotels.

Standing across the street, the man who called himself Joey C. Brenner studied it for twenty seconds. Then he looked both left and right to get a better sense of the neighborhood—in case he had to leave in a hurry.

If he played it wrong, he'd have to.

Unless they carried him out in a garbage bag.

Recognizing a man of authority, the doorman nodded to him deferentially as he approached the entrance. Brenner walked into the lobby, swiftly scanned its layout and exits, and made his way to the elevators. Their polished brass doors had the same tone of aged elegance that lent the whole hotel its air of stylish solidity and affluence.

How deceptive appearance can be, Brenner reflected as he pressed the call button. When the door opened, he found himself facing the operator standing beside the control panel.

"Down," Brenner said.

"No *down* in this elevator, sir," the operator announced.

"A hundred says there is," Brenner replied. As he spoke, he thrust a hundred-dollar bill at the man and flipped open his own jacket to show that he had neither badge nor shoulder holster.

"I'm a player," he assured the security-minded operator.

Even though he didn't offer the password, his cash and affable manner combined to win him access to the basement that supposedly didn't exist. To be precise, it was a subbasement, and it was *something*.

The large chamber was furnished and decorated in eye-catching ultramodern everything—lots of metallic items, leather, razzle-dazzle contemporary lighting fixtures, and a lavish use of bold colors. The gambling equipment was roulette wheels; tables for baccarat, poker, and craps; and a half dozen slot machines set to accept the house's electronically coded ten-dollar chips.

This was one of Carl Rocca's best houses—hidden under a "superior" and long-established hotel, and designed to attract "civilized" gamblers with plenty of money and polish. It was light-years away from the Lamansky operation that collapsed with its ceiling and roof when the tow truck pulled out the central support column.

The customers here were male and female executives, lawyers, bankers, stockbrokers, top doctors, and real-estate magnates—and their consorts. Everyone was fashionably and expensively dressed. Though a number of the women wore clothes from top stores and impressive jewelry, there was no "flash" here. This was the Establishment.

Brenner looked around, searching the room for the Right Man. He didn't know who he was or what he looked like, but he would recognize him when he saw him. He'd be looking around too.

There he was.

Large and vigilant.

About six-foot-three and nearly two hundred forty pounds, he wore a tuxedo and a watchful expression. Standing against the wall as he surveyed the room, the man was plainly part of the gaming establishment's staff. He might even be captain of the defensive team, the "dead" sheriff reckoned.

It was time for Joey C. Brenner to make his move.

He smiled as he reached the man in the tuxedo.

"Good evening. What do you need?" the casino employee asked cheerfully.

Whatever it was—animal, vegetable, or mineral—you could get it here. Cocaine or gambling credit, a fine thirty-year-old Armagnac, or a pair of twin sixteen-year-old sisters— all these and *much* more were available to keep the rich clientele content.

A satisfied customer returns.

A gambler who comes back loses more.

Simple mathematics.

"I need five minutes with Carl Rocca," Brenner said.

The man in the tuxedo looked him over swiftly.

Not a regular customer. Not visibly rich.

"Afraid that's not possible," he answered.

"Try. Tell him I'm the big pain in Ben Lamansky's fat ass."

The big man eyed him appraisingly again.

"Wait here," he said, and walked away.

Brenner nodded. In a little while he strolled fifteen yards to a baccarat table where eight people were playing intently. A woman had "the shoe." She was long-legged and lovely with fine features and a mane of pale golden hair. Her figure was arresting, her troubled blue eyes even more so.

She was a beautiful woman but a bad gambler, handling the cards with an impatience that had to defeat her. It did. She lost hand after hand. After a while she noticed that Brenner was watching her. For some reason she didn't quite understand, this handsome man made her feel self-conscious. She didn't like it.

"Losing improves your character," she said defiantly.

"But winning improves your wardrobe," he answered.

"You don't like mine?"

The elegant silver sheath fit her like a second skin, presenting her extraordinary figure in stunning splendor. The guys who designed the Golden Gate Bridge must have created that cantilevered bra for her, Brenner thought.

"No, it's perfect," he admitted.

Her eyes followed him for a few seconds as he moved on. Then she went back to losing more chips.

Brenner looked across the room, saw the big man in the tuxedo beckon, and sauntered coolly through the crowd to join him. The ex-FBI agent followed him up a corridor to a steel door that his escort opened with a key. Some dozen yards beyond was another metal-sheathed door with a closed-circuit TV camera on the wall beside it.

The casino man rapped on the door. Five seconds later there was a whirring noise as the camera turned to scan them. Then they heard a hum, and the electrically controlled barrier swung open.

"Come in!" a voice inside ordered harshly.

Those gravelly tones were familiar. The undercover cop had heard them in the command and control bunker at Camp LeJeune. They belonged to Carl Rocca.

One wall of the office was adorned with eighteen TV screens connected to closed-circuit security cameras in the casino. Facing them behind a huge and costly teak desk was Luigi Patrovita's right-hand man and primary enforcer, Carl Rocca.

Same loud, expensive clothes.

Now he was wearing a two-carat diamond pinky ring in addition to the big gold Rolex wristwatch—and a look of calculating curiosity. The expression on the thirty-seven-year-old hoodlum standing beside him was quite different. As usual, hard-faced Max Keller was glaring in perpetual hostility. According to FBI reports, he was even cruder and meaner than his seated boss. It figured. He was the muscle man's muscle man.

"What's your name?" Rocca demanded.

"Joseph C. Brenner. They call me Joey."

"So you're the guy who's been giving Lamansky a hard time, huh? Wrecked one of his joints...grabbed his Caddy—"

"And his chick's jewelry," Brenner said. "Here it is."

He took a paper bag from his pocket, emptied it on the desk.

"Why did you do that, Joey?" Rocca tested.

"To shake him up...let him know nothing he's got is safe."

"What the hell you trying to prove, sonny?" Keller sneered.

There was no cheer in his smile. It was thin and sharp—like a dagger. Suddenly the air was thick with tension and bitterness.

"Joey, this is Max Keller. He takes care of all kinds of things for me," Rocca announced.

"You didn't answer my question, sonny," Keller said nastily.

"I'm trying to prove Mr. Rocca might be able to use me."

"For what?" Carl Rocca asked.

"To take care of things—all kinds of things."

"That's a *man's* job, sonny," Keller mocked, "and it's filled."

"I figure a smart person like Mr. Rocca might be looking for something better."

Keller stepped forward threateningly.

"It don't get any better than *me*," he declared.

"It's got to," the muscular newcomer answered calmly.

That ripped it. Keller grimaced in rage, charged forward, and swung with all his might at the insulting stranger's jaw. His foe stepped aside with easy grace, grabbed Keller's wrist, and expertly rotated it. In seconds Keller's face was white with terrible pain. Hurt coursed through his whole body as Joey Brenner scientifically and inexorably forced him to his knees.

Rocca watched with professional interest as his widely feared strongarm ace writhed . . . gasped . . . and finally yelped in agony.

"You gotta watch your temper," Brenner told the thug he was humiliating. "Learn new ways to let off steam. If I had the time, *sonny,* I'd teach you how to roll over and play real dead."

Having made his point, he released his hold. A second later the livid hoodlum grabbed under his jacket for his gun. The "dead" sheriff instantly raised his hammer fist to break his shoulder.

He didn't have to.

"Hold it, Max!" Rocca shouted.

Keller froze.

"What the hell you think my office is—a goddamn shooting gallery? You lost your mind?"

Still tingling with pain and burning to get even, Keller silently struggled to his feet and retreated—glaring at the poker-faced enemy who'd shamed and hurt him so easily. Rocca was looking at him too.

"Tell me, Joey. What makes you think I could be lookin' for a new boy?" the man behind the desk asked.

"Nothin' special, Mr. Rocca. Just thought I might get lucky."

"I know you're not local. Where you from?"

"The last few years, Miami."

"References?"

"The best—the feds. I'm in their lousy computer. A top guy like you has to own a cop or two, and they can punch out my record for you in ten seconds."

So he wasn't just strong and fast, Rocca thought. He had a head as well as fists. Might be a real find.

"Who told you I'd be happy to see Snake Lamansky's ass kicked?" Rocca probed craftily.

"Coke's king down in Miami," Joey Brenner replied. "You can tell anything and everything by the flow of the blow. Lamansky's making bigger buys each week, and that takes a load of cash. Where's he getting all that bread? I figure he's bitin' into somebody else's action. Since your operation is number one in Lamansky's hometown, I figure he's cuttin' in on you."

Rocca nodded.

"You got a big rep, Mr. Rocca. Everybody knows that you and your people don't take crap from nobody," the infiltrator continued earnestly. "If this dirt bag's botherin' you, I figure you'd like to piss on his parade too."

"You figure pretty good," Rocca told him. "Tell the cashier to give you a grand in chips—my compliments. Enjoy yourself."

"Thanks. Don't want to bug you, but what about the job?"

Rocca shrugged.

"Maybe you'll hear from me," he announced grandly. "Don't forget your jewelry, Joey."

"I don't want it. I want to work for you."

"He's got class," Rocca said after Joey Brenner followed the man in the tuxedo out and the steel door closed.

"It's a con," the still smarting Max Keller argued. "I don't believe a fuckin' word he told you. He might be a spy for Lamansky, you know. This whole bit could be a setup for another hit!"

Yeah, it was possible.

The Snake was a tricky bastard.

"I'll get the book on Joseph C. Brenner from that fed computer," Rocca declared. "We'll check him out from top to bottom."

"Why not just tell him to screw off now?" Keller urged. "Hell, we don't need him."

"If he's what he claims, you always need a guy like that. It's like saving for a rainy day, Max. You know—something that could come in handy in the future."

Rocca was disappointed to see that Keller didn't seem to understand. He'd never rise higher. The poor son of a bitch never thought ahead—a basic thing for a businessman. He'd always be muscle with no hope for advancement into management.

Out in the casino Amy Kaminski's husband collected his thousand dollars in chips and went to watch the beautiful blonde at the baccarat table. He played beside her—skillfully and patiently. Within ten minutes he'd doubled his money— and she kept losing.

"I don't think anybody'd mind if you went home before you were broke," he prodded gently.

"Don't worry about my money," she snapped. "I have friends here. I can always get more."

He pushed all his chips over to her and rose.

"Try some of mine," he invited. "It might change your luck."

She waited for the inevitable "pass."

She'd been around long enough to know that men didn't give pretty young women two thousand dollars without expecting something in return.

What did this one want?

He didn't say. He walked away without saying another word. When he reached the street above, he felt the cool breeze sweeping in from Lake Michigan. It would soon be winter. Where would he be when the snow began to fall?

Inside the Patrovita gang . . . back with his wife . . . or at the bottom of one of the Great Lakes?

He glanced up and down the street again—just in case Lamansky's gunners might be waiting. After a few seconds he turned right, heading north. The two armed men in the gray car across the street near the corner watched as he zigzagged through the flowing stream of pedestrians.

The older of the pair was in his forties, with patches of gray at the temples to prove it. He'd seen it all and hadn't liked most of it. Ira Baker's friends called him Tommy because he'd once taken a submachine gun from someone trying to kill him and redecorated the assassin's face with the butt. The other man in the sedan—Joel Carson—was both more eager and more tense. Being twenty-seven is rarely without sideeffects.

Now they saw three men leave the hotel. The trio was easy to identify. Their expressions, clothes, stances, and body language were quite clear to any expert.

"Goons," Baker said matter-of-factly.

After nineteen years on the Chicago PD, he was a tough and savvy expert on the basic varieties of hoodlum. Tommy Baker despised them all.

He watched them look around and saw them nod toward the former FBI agent. Some fifty yards away from them, Joey Brenner strolled on, pausing only to check the knot of his tie in the side mirror of a parked delivery van.

He spotted them at once.

He saw them watching him intently, and he made up his mind.

Joey Brenner sauntered on a dozen yards before turning up the alley beside a French restaurant. The fragrant smells of garlic and herbs reminded him of his wife's favorite dining place in New York, and the acute gastronomic limitations of Barrett, North Carolina.

He walked slowly—as if he didn't have a care. He listened carefully—because he did. The hoodlums were following him up the alley. He could hear their footsteps drawing closer. Time for act two.

He stopped, turned, and did his best to look frightened. They took the bait and advanced swiftly.

He spun on his heel . . . ran. They raced after him.

When he turned the corner of the twisting alley, he stopped dead in his tracks and pressed himself against the wall. He raised his arm, the hard-edged side of his hand facing out in the attack position. Totally alert and coiled to strike, he waited for the thugs to turn the corner.

The thin, swarthy one was the first. He was utterly surprised when the hard-edged hand smashed him in the forehead. A two-inch cut opened up, and the dazed hoodlum went down onto the urban carpet of gum and garbage.

He screamed as he fell, but no one was interested. The second hoodlum nearly tripped over him. Recovering his balance, the burly goon pulled a blackjack from his pocket and lifted it to strike. A karate chop that broke his forearm made him drop it with a howl. The kick to his stomach three seconds later knocked the wind out of him so he couldn't scream. He doubled over, reeled back grunting.

The third man got in one punch before Brenner could give him his full attention. It caught the ex-FBI operative on the left ear. Brenner shattered his shoulder with a blindingly fast chop and then stunned him with a blow to the temple, which filled his whole head with dizzying hurt.

The first one was on his feet again. This time he had a wild look of hatred in his mad-dog eyes and a switchblade in his left hand. He clicked it open with a triumphant leer.

Brenner eyed him calmly.

"Next of kin?" he asked.

The man with the knife looked puzzled.

"Where do we send the remains?" Brenner questioned.

Then he noticed that the thug with the blackjack was raising it again, so he caught him by the wrist and sent him crashing headfirst into a brick wall.

A siren sounded. A car with a flashing light on top suddenly appeared at the far end of the alley.

"Cops!" the man with the knife shouted. His partners lurched to their feet and fled out the other way. Brenner straightened his clothes as he watched them go. Then he turned and started toward the vehicle with the flashing light.

The two plainclothes detectives got out of the unmarked police car. The older man leaned against it, studying the scene. The younger detective warily drew his gun. After a few seconds the senior detective lit a cigarette and walked to meet Amy Kaminski's husband.

"Any trouble, mister?" Baker asked.

"Not really. Every city has a rat problem."

The veteran detective nodded . . . puffed on his cigarette.

"What did those guys want?" he asked.

"Hard to say. We never had time to discuss it."

Whoever he was, the bastard was cool.

"Mind showing some ID?" the policeman queried.

Brenner reached into his jacket slowly, took out his wallet, and flipped it open.

"Don't mind at all, Officer," he said as he passed it to the detective.

"Joseph C. Brenner. What does the C. stand for?"

"Clean," the muscular stranger replied, and drew open his jacket to show that he had no shoulder-holstered gun.

Very cool and rock-hard.

Who was Joseph C. Brenner?

Had it been a routine mugging attempt or something else?

"Stay clean, Mr. Brenner," the thoughtful plainclothes cop advised as he handed back the wallet.

"Always do, Officer."

The two detectives got back into their car and drove away.

Their showing up hadn't been mere coincidence, Mark Kaminski reasoned.

They'd been on surveillance duty. Watching the hotel-casino or Joey Brenner?

Were they honest police on official business or crooked cops spying for Lamansky—lining up targets for his hit men? They were undoubtedly looking for "Joey," and the price a furious Ben Lamansky must have put on his head.

The man who called himself Joey C. Brenner was right in the goddamn middle, and he'd be there for a while. Well, he'd been there before. He walked to the street, double-checked for any sign of watchers, and made his way to an ice-cream parlor three blocks away. Such fare wasn't on his usual diet, but the chocolate-chocolate chip was delicious.

Then he returned to his rented apartment and did two hundred push-ups before he took a hot shower and went to bed. When he closed his eyes, he saw the face of the woman he'd left in North Carolina. It was nearly one A.M. when he finally fell asleep.

21

Five hours later . . . six and a half miles away.

A middle-class neighborhood of "good" private homes on a clean, quiet street. Almost all these houses were owned by hardworking and respectable couples with combined earnings of fifty or sixty thousand dollars.

One wasn't.

It belonged to a corporation owned by a holding company controlled by a dummy firm that existed only as a mailing address in the Bahamas. Its annual income was in the tens of millions.

Its tenants of record were Mr. and Mrs. Barry Fittel. He worked for an accounting firm, and she was employed by a toy wholesaler with a showroom in The Loop. It was all a lie. They weren't tenants, and neither of them was named Fittel. Not a penny of the thousand dollars a week each received came from accounting or toys.

In the back of a parked tan van adorned with a Disneyland '85 bumper sticker, Detective Sergeant Ira Baker drained his carton of tepid coffee and looked at his watch. The men inside 104 Sloan Terrace would be tired by now. They'd been working all night. This was the time to attack.

He adjusted the Kevlar bulletproof vest that made him itch, loosened the Police Special in his belly holster, and picked up the walkie-talkie.

"Showtime . . . repeat, showtime," he said into the radio.

There was still some night mist on Sloan Terrace. A very attractive young brunette in the "right" jogging attire trotted through the last wisps of fog, splashing through puddles now and then with the dedication of the conscientious fitness addict. Wearing a jaunty sweatband and figure-hugging running suit, she looked both healthy and sexy as she approached the green sedan parked in front of the "Fittel" house.

There was a red-eyed man behind the wheel.

He'd been there for almost two hours.

In another ten minutes another man would replace him. The bored sentry hoped that he'd be on time. The lookout's kidneys were sending unmistakable messages.

She stopped beside the driver's window, smiled *very* seductively, and leaned closer to speak.

What a great piece! he thought lewdly for a moment.

He changed his mind when she produced a compact .32 automatic and shoved it near his face.

About four inches away.

"Let's hop in and get some coffee," she said sweetly.

Realizing that it was more of a command than an invitation, he yielded. If she was a cop, she wouldn't shoot him. If she worked with some other mob here for a rip-off, she'd blow his brains out. He decided to play it safe.

He had a walkie-talkie too. It rested on the seat beside him. He lifted it slowly and cleared his tight throat before he spoke.

"It's Ernie. I'm coming . . . to take a leak."

"Good thinking, Ernie," she complimented as he got out of the car. "I like that bit about the leak. I'll put in a word with the D.A. for you."

He immediately thought of several great things to say. "Screw the D.A." and "Up yours, lady" were two of them. But it might not be prudent to utter either remark to someone pointing a .32 at your head. Since she'd mentioned the D.A., she was *probably* a cop—and wouldn't blast him. But *probably* wasn't good enough, so he kept his anger to himself.

Feeling nervous and depressed, he trudged toward the house with the counterfeit jogger one step behind him. His eyes were on the door. He didn't notice the armed men drifting silently out of the mist. There were more than a dozen. Another nine were closing in on 104 Sloan Terrace from the rear.

In the ground-floor living room four contemptible men sat working around a large table. Wearing gauze masks and white cotton gloves, they were measuring and bagging heroin in small plastic envelopes. At a smaller table a few feet away another greedy criminal was "cutting" a fresh supply to reduce the purity and increase the bulk and profits. He had a mask and gloves too.

The two men on the couch and the one slumped in the overstuffed armchair didn't. One had a .357 Magnum in a belly holster, the others 38-caliber pistols in canvas slings under their arms. This trio—the same men who'd tried to maim Joey Brenner in the alley—were the security team.

There were other weapons in the room. Three submachine guns and a U.S. Army M16 leaned against one wall. A pair of repeating shotguns and a rapid-fire Ingram M-11 rested against another, held up by boxes of ammunition. There was little conversation. Weary after long hours of work, everyone wanted to finish the shift and go to sleep.

When they heard "Ernie' unlock the front door, they barely glanced toward the sound. A split second later many other noises—much louder—filled the house. It was the assault team of narcotics cops smashing in doors and windows in a lightning raid.

His .38 in hand and ready to fire, Ira Baker was the first to break into the front hall. He shoved "Ernie" aside and bounded into the doorway to the living room. In impulsive reaction the hoodlum who had tried to hack up Brenner with a switchblade grabbed for the M16.

"Freeze!" Baker yelled.

The hoodlum hesitated, his hand inches from the weapon.

"Go ahead, moron. Do it!" the detective urged in a voice jagged with hostility.

The words didn't matter.

The look in his eyes said it all.

Another inch and you're dead.

The mob's security man pulled back his hand, slowly and carefully. He was fully aware that this was one of those hair-trigger cops, the kind who'd blow him away at the slightest excuse. Embittered by the excellent legal services that rich gang bosses such as Patrovita provided, those police were looking for a reason to shoot the mob guys whom the courts couldn't hold.

"You got no right to bust in like this," another thug complained. "Not without a paper."

"Here it is," Baker replied, and pulled a folded document from his jacket. "I got the warrant, and Lou Patrovita's got a lot of trouble."

"What about us?"

"You've got a nice chance to do five to ten—if you live that long. The Emperor doesn't appreciate jerks who let the cops take his goods."

Then Ira Baker saw the third table in the corner. It was

eight feet long and a yard wide. Every inch of the surface was covered.

"Oh, my God!" Baker gasped.

Heaped across the entire top of the worktable was money. Stacks and stacks and more stacks of U.S. currency. Fives and tens and twenties piled two feet high . . . fifties and hundreds tied in three-inch bundles that rose even higher.

There were millions of dollars on the table.

Ira Baker had never seen anything like it.

"Read them their rights, will you?" he asked another of the raiders.

"And what the hell will you do?" the other cop grumbled.

"Call the president," Detective Sergeant Ira Baker declared exuberantly. "There's great news. I think the Chicago Police Department just fixed the national deficit."

22

Big money.

It was written all over the large and elaborately furnished office.

Everything was ultramodern, top-of-the-line, and visibly expensive.

This was Luigi Patrovita's executive suite—the throne room of one of the reigning monarchs of the underworld. This sovereign had connections, investments, and power on every continent. He was no mere local warlord who ruled Chicago and some nearby parts of the U.S. Midwest. He was a global force.

And he was livid.

"Are you out of your stinkin' mind?" he blazed as he ground out an expensive and illegally imported Cuban cigar. "What the hell's the matter with you? Your brain up your ass or something?"

Rocca tried to answer.

The Emperor didn't let him.

"I ain't surprised by this—just disgusted," he declared angrily. "How long you been using that goddamn house?"

"Not long."

"*How long,* dammit?"

"Three or four months. Maybe four and a half," Rocca admitted.

"Every baby who still craps in his diaper knows that's too long. I told you a hundred times—eight weeks is max. And what's the damage?"

"Cash—a little over sixteen million."

Patrovita shook his head and scowled.

"And merchandise?" he asked.

"The wholesalers were coming by in a couple of hours, Lou."

"What the fuck are you saying?"

"We hadn't dropped *any* of it," Rocca told him. "They got it *all.*"

"That horse is worth eighty million bucks on the street, Carl," Patrovita said grimly.

"I know, but we can replace it in a couple a weeks."

Patrovita's fist slammed onto the top of the desk.

"Couple a weeks? Lamansky's not going to give us a couple a weeks," he predicted. "If he's got a lot of stuff—like we hear—he'll step into our territories with bargain prices."

"Our customers won't play with him," Rocca protested.

"You can bet your ass they will if we can't supply them. That ambitious bastard will take a big chunk of our business— and it won't be that easy to get it back."

The hoodlum Harry Shannon had called The Undertaker refused to be discouraged.

"Why don't we just take Lamansky out?" he proposed.

Patrovita impatiently bit the tip off another five-dollar cigar and lit it.

"Easy to say . . . hard to do. He'll be looking for it, Carl.

Has been since his boys blew that bus job. We'll bury him later. Now gimme the rest of the bad news."

"Not so bad," Rocca answered. "Eight of our guys got busted at the house, but nobody pulled a trigger. They'll all make bail by morning."

"When they do, ask them how it happened. I want answers—or heads. We can't afford guys who screw up—not with that bastard Lamansky out to hit me. You find a replacement for Tony yet?"

"Maybe. I'm looking someone over."

"Look *fast*," Patrovita ordered irritably.

Rocca nodded.

"Anything else?" he asked.

Several seconds passed before The Emperor answered.

"Yeah . . . I want it back . . . all of it."

"All *what*?" Carl Rocca questioned in the gravelly voice.

"Every goddamn thing that went this morning. The sixteen million . . . the smack too. It's mine."

Rocca looked stunned.

"I paid for it," Patrovita said, "so I own it. Get it, Carl."

It was a monarch's edict, blunt and nonnegotiable.

"Gonna be tough, Lou. We don't even know where the damn cops have it."

Patrovita took out another big cigar and lit it with the gold Dunhill.

"We got a friend who can find out," he reminded Rocca. "He'll tell me and I'll tell you."

"Jeezus, Lou, they could have it in a vault in the police commissioner's office downtown. You can't just blast your way in there."

His words had no impact at all.

It was as if he hadn't spoken.

"When I tell you, you'll get it," Patrovita decreed. "I'll let you know as soon as I hear."

Then he picked up the telephone, and Rocca understood that he had been dismissed. When he reached the outer office, he saw the five-foot-nine-inch Eurasian woman who came to Patrovita's office three times a week.

Every Monday, Wednesday, and Friday at four in the afternoon. She was a young woman with old and knowing eyes. She always arrived with a box crafted of polished ebony—two feet long, four inches wide, and five inches high.

Rocca looked at the box. As he had so many times before, he wondered what was in it. What happened in Luigi Patrovita's office each Monday, Wednesday, and Friday afternoon between four and five?

A buzzer sounded, and Patrovita's male secretary pressed the switch that opened the door to The Emperor's inner office. The woman with the box entered, and Carl Rocca went out to arrange bail for the eight men captured in the raid.

As the private elevator descended from the penthouse suite Rocca noticed the exotic scent in the air. It was some kind of jasmine—the Eurasian woman's perfume. That was probably all he'd ever know about her, he thought. He had no idea what her name was or even if she spoke English.

Then he found himself considering the puzzle of the shiny black box again . . . and shook his head. Carl Rocca decided that he'd better forget about that box. Why waste time thinking about it? He would *never* learn what it held.

When he reached his car, he turned his attention to something more practical and immediate: the question of Joey Brenner. He was still thinking about the swift and strong young stranger when he entered the underground casino eighteen minutes later.

23

The furnished apartment that the ex-FBI agent had rented
was nothing to write home about.

Not even a postcard.

It was small, and the wall color matched the furniture
quite nicely. Both were Contemporary Dull with interesting
touches of Tired and Uncomfortable. The place was clean,
perhaps because it was too dreary to interest roaches.

To be fair, there was plenty of sunlight and the phono-
stereo set wasn't too bad. The record machine was playing
now, filling the living-dining room with the thunder of
Brahms. Stripped to the waist, the man who called himself
Joey Brenner finished his daily ten minutes of running in
place. It was a regular part of his aerobic program, but these
exercises weren't enough to stay in *top* condition. Tomorrow
he'd buy some weights.

Having completed the running, he mopped the sweat from
his face and upper torso with a terry-cloth towel and decided
to call Harry Shannon. It was time for "the corpse" to
report. He reached for the telephone . . . paused . . . and pulled
back his hand.

He had nearly made an elementary and possibly fatal error.

If Rocca was checking him out, there was a good chance that some of The Emperor's numerous soldiers had found out where he lived. They might be watching the apartment— or tapping the phone—now.

Someone was watching.

He wasn't that good, either.

Joey Brenner spotted the man in the dark blue raincoat within a minute after leaving the apartment house. He led the watcher down the street, bought a copy of the final edition of the *Tribune*, and strolled on to study shirts in a men's store window on the next block.

Some thirty yards beyond the clothing shop stood a phone booth. Brenner sauntered up to it, entered, and dialed the safe house's number, which he'd memorized. After two rings Shannon's recorded voice sounded in his ear.

"Hello, you have reached the Wilkses. Pearl and I can't talk to you now, so please leave your message when you hear the electronic beep."

"So far, so good," Brenner reported five seconds later as he eyed the watcher across the street. "I've been kicking ass all over town, and a lot of people would like to wreck mine. I've met your cousin at the undertaking parlor. We spoke about a job, and I think he's checking my references right now. I'll call you as soon as I hear. *Ciao.*"

As he walked back to the apartment house he wondered who employed the man following him.

Rocca?

Lamansky?

Local law—or someone else?

It might even be Max Keller, still out for vengeance.

Probably Carl Rocca. That made the most sense. It was

only an educated guess, of course. It had better be a right one. If it was wrong, it could be his last.

He walked on slowly. He was nearly "home" when he decided not to return to the apartment. There was something else he had to do. A high-powered hoodlum from Miami with plenty of cash wouldn't just wander the streets on foot. He'd get some "flash" wheels to impress people—including himself.

In any business, in any social circle, in any country, the "right" car mattered. It was stupid, the imitation gangster thought, but it was one of the facts of life. Men and women and bank presidents and professors and mobsters would all take him more seriously if his vehicle was "important."

So he made his way to a Hertz branch and rented a big Cadillac town car. He smiled as he drove it away. There was still the *possibility* that Rocca would find out that he was a fake and send killers—but something else was quite certain.

If they "hit" Kaminski behind the wheel of his car, he'd go out in style.

24

*A*t eleven-forty that night Joey Brenner returned to the posh underground gambling casino and told a security man that Mr. Rocca wanted to see him. Five minutes later he faced Carl Rocca in the office where they'd met before.

Max Keller sat on a small couch against the wall.

He still looked as nasty as a toothache.

"What makes you think I want to see you, Joey?" Rocca asked.

"Well, Mr. Rocca, you're a very important man with very heavy connections. I figured that those connections must have checked me out real good by now," Brenner announced, "so I thought I'd fall by to see if I got the job."

"You wanted to save me the phone call?" Rocca smirked.

"Just trying to be helpful."

"I think you might, Joey. You're right about those connections. I got the whole damn story on you—and I'm impressed. How the hell is it you never did time?"

"I'm almost as careful as you are," Brenner answered, "and I'm tricky. It runs in the family."

He heard Keller curse softly from the couch.

"Max thinks you're *too* tricky," Rocca said, "but I'm gonna give you a chance. If you screw up, Max won't. You'll be working with him. He'll show you the ropes."

And hang me with them if he gets a chance, Brenner thought.

"Let's try it for a month to see if you're the guy I want," Rocca continued. "If you are, it's five grand a month. Do a good job and there'll be more."

"I'll do a *great* job. Thanks, Mr. Rocca. When do I start?"

"Tomorrow," Rocca replied, and gestured to Keller to see the new recruit out.

In the corridor outside, Keller eyed him coldly.

"If you need a piece, say so."

"Thanks, but I got my own."

Suddenly a .38 bloomed in his hand—as if by magic.

"Not bad," Keller admitted. "Do you know how to use it?"

"Yeah—I've had a lot of practice."

Keller walked him back to the casino.

"Noon tomorrow—here. Don't be late," the hoodlum said, and strode off toward the bar.

Joseph C. Brenner made his way to the street. He gave the doorman the claim check for his car—and felt pleased. He'd passed through the first barrier. He was wondering what they'd assign him to do tomorrow when he saw the dazzling, slim blonde emerge from the hotel. She wasn't wearing the silver sheath tonight, but she still looked stunning.

"Taxi, Sam—please," she said to the doorman.

"How'd you make out the other night?" Carl Rocca's newest employee asked.

"Your cash didn't change a thing."

"Tonight?"

She shook her head and smiled ruefully.

"Maybe you should try another kind of recreation," Brenner told her.

"Any suggestions?"

"You might try physical exercise. A good workout might be great."

She studied his extraordinary physique.

"Maybe it might," she agreed with a widening smile.

Then his Cadillac arrived, and he opened the door for her.

"Your car, ma'am," he said with a flourish.

"My name's Monique. Monique Tyler."

"Joseph C. Brenner at your service. C stands for clean," he announced cheerily.

An hour and a half and two bottles of Mumm's Cordon Rouge later, they sat on the floor of his living room—both of them aglow with the effects of good champagne. His jacket and tie were draped over an adjacent armchair, and his shirt was unbuttoned to mid-chest.

Her shoes were off, her hair was mussed, and her skirt was hiked up above her knees—but she didn't care. It was almost time for the exercise. The anticipation made her smile again.

"These bubbles really put you out," Brenner said, tipsy. "I'm ready for bed."

"What a great idea!" she replied, and they both giggled.

He had drunk a lot more champagne than she had, and it showed. He was unsteady when he got to his feet. He leaned on her as they made their way to the next room—a chamber dominated by a large brass bed.

Brenner pointed to the bed with a swaying hand.

"Perfect for aerobics," he announced.

"And other things," she answered as she began to undo the remaining buttons of his shirt. When the last one was opened, she helped him slip out of the garment. She had never seen such a perfectly conditioned man's body before.

"*Fantastic!*" she whispered in a choked voice that blended admiration and desire.

This male animal made the much publicized TV "hunks" look like gilded wimps. Unable to keep her hands off him, she rushed to kiss and embrace him. They kissed long and hard . . . then soft and tender. She felt stirrings deep within. It was time.

She undressed quickly, but it was too late.

The surfeit of champagne had put him to sleep.

Disappointment, anger, frustration, resignation coursed through her as she contemplated the most physically perfect and attractive man she'd ever seen. It wasn't right. It wasn't fair.

Then she sighed and remembered what she had agreed to do. She might as well get it over with. Naked, she padded out to the living room to pull his wallet from the pocket of his jacket. With his snores echoing from the bedroom she picked up the telephone and dialed.

"I'm at his place. Take this down. Joseph C. Brenner, Social Security number 567-34-5787. Florida driver's license number 487368929. He's got a passport and a pistol permit too."

Brenner was still snoring, but he wasn't asleep. He never had been. He was standing just out of sight in the dimly lit bedroom, listening to every word.

"4309," she said, repeating the final digits of the handgun license. "No, I can't speak louder. Don't want to wake him. . . . Now that's a thousand of my IOUs you're cancelling, right? . . . Yeah. . . . If I get anything else, I'll call."

The conversation was clearly about to end. The "dead" sheriff hurried back to the bed to lie down again—snoring steadily as he moved. He found the same position that he'd been in before—and continued listening. His hearing was as well developed as his biceps.

"Watch your mouth!" she said indignantly. "You can't talk to me like that! If you think—"

She stopped speaking.

The smug racketeer at the other end of the line had simply hung up on her. She sat there with the instrument in her hand, the insistent dial tone her only companion as she considered her dilemma.

After a dozen seconds the nude woman walked back to the bedroom to look at the extraordinary man sprawled on the bed. It wasn't just his physical attributes that made him unusual. He'd been kind and decent—respectful. For the first time in years she'd found a man who didn't treat her like a whore, and she was behaving like one, anyway.

It was ironic, she reflected.

And it was unfair.

Joey Brenner was the sort of man she could love, and he might have loved her too.

It might have been *wonderful,* she thought with a sigh. Then she lay down beside him, basking in his nearness and body heat. The champagne finally took effect, and she escaped into the blackness of deep sleep.

25

She was gone when he awoke the next morning.

The watcher in the blue raincoat wasn't.

Brenner—he *had* to think of himself as hoodlum Joey Brenner—wondered whether the man had been standing out there all night. He'd been on long surveillance shifts himself, and he couldn't help sympathizing with the poor bastard a little.

Not much.

Whoever he was, the watcher was almost surely an enemy.

As Brenner ate his breakfast of wheat germ and unsugared bran flakes, he began to speculate on what his first day on the new job would be like. At least there wouldn't be any damn forms to fill out—a blessing. Both Mark Kaminski and Joey Brenner hated forms and paperwork—one of the few things they had in common.

Brenner would have to be cool and careful with Max. He'd avoid confrontations . . . let Max take the lead as the senior employee who knew the setup. Brenner couldn't be weak or let Max Keller walk over him, but he'd play it low-key and steady. Keller already hated his guts and was waiting for any excuse to spill them. Keller would enjoy that.

Max Keller was a psycho thug and murderer who loved his work. His sickness was written all over him. He probably strangled kittens as a hobby, the ex-FBI agent thought as he drained his orange juice. Mobsters such as Keller had no limits.

He'd be testing all the time, pushing the new man to see how far he'd go and probing for any weaknesses. Every hour of every day would be tricky with this bitter bastard, but hard-boiled Joey Brenner from Miami could handle him. He'd dealt with other violent vermin, and he'd cope with this rabid animal too.

It was entirely possible that Brenner would find himself in a situation where he had to shoot it out with the hate-filled psycho. If he had to do that, he would. That didn't worry him. More troubling was the risk that the mobsters would give him an assignment that brought him into head-on collision with the police.

Eyeball to eyeball.

Down the barrel of a gun.

What would he do if he faced a pistol or machine gun in the hands of some cop who was about to squeeze the trigger? Joey Brenner would blow the policeman away without hesitation. If he didn't, the cop might kill him. Even in the crazy eighties it would be the ultimate irony to be gunned down by a fellow lawman.

Kaminski or Brenner—did it *really* matter? People said that humans' strongest instinct was for survival. Would that primitive passion—fundamental and born in his bones—prevail over his morality and loyalty to the police family? How far would a man—not a saint—go to save his own life?

That was only half of the dilemma, Amy Kaminski's husband brooded as he carried the dishes to the sink. It might be just as dangerous if he didn't shoot at the cop. Keller or Rocca might realize that he wasn't the ruthless hoodlum he was pretending to be. That could be fatal too.

Watch your step, Joey, Kaminski thought grimly.

If he was going to pass as Brenner, he'd have to think like Brenner. He glanced out the window again, saw the watcher, and made up his mind.

Sure.

He'd have to find the right place. He picked up yesterday's newspaper, flipped the pages to the entertainment section, and found what he was looking for. Then he checked the clip in the .38, slid the gun into his shoulder holster and put on his jacket and coat. It ought to work, he calculated as he left the apartment.

Some fifteen minutes later he parked the Cadillac in a downtown lot and walked three blocks to the movie theater whose ad he'd seen.

THREE HOT FEATURES!
SWEDISH TRAMPS!
NYMPHO WEEKEND!
GIMME MORE!

As he bought the ticket he caught a glimpse of the watcher reflected in the window of the cashier's booth. The bored cashier—a dead ringer for Whistler's mother in the famous painting—gave him his change and went back to studying the *Wall Street Journal*. Brenner entered the porno theater and waited for his eyes to adjust to the semi-darkness.

After a minute he sat down. There were about fifty

men—and one woman—in the chamber. There were three couples on the screen. No, there were half a dozen under-nourished people with bad skin and worse voices up there *coupling*.

In various ways.

In changing combinations.

And the crappy rock-music track was outstandingly terrible.

Kaminski hadn't chosen this theater because he liked sex films. He'd picked it because: one, regular movie houses weren't open this early; and two, the carnal capers on the screen might divert the watcher's attention.

They did.

When the cast expanded to ten—including a cross-eyed woman who appeared to be a retired wet nurse and a short Latin male in an ill-fitting toupee, Kaminski made his move. He turned, saw that the watcher was completely focused on the movie. Kaminski slid slowly to the side aisle, made sure that his "tail" was still staring at the picture, and circled around to the row behind him.

The epic's director must have been a square-dance enthu-siast, for people kept changing partners at forty-five-second intervals. One redheaded female was yelping conscientiously to show interest.

A nice touch, Kaminski thought as he reached forward and delivered a numbing chop to the back of the neck that left the watcher unconscious. He'd stay that way for at least an hour.

Having terminated the surveillance—as Joey Brenner would in one way or another, the former FBI agent left the theater. He arrived at the subterranean casino exactly at noon, as instructed.

Keller didn't show up until twelve twenty-five, and he spoke just one word.

"Wait."

Then he swaggered away into a back room, leaving Joey C. Brenner to sit there while cleaning women mopped the floor around him. The thug probably wouldn't return for half an hour, Brenner guessed. This whole deal was a clumsy demonstration of power . . . a petty attempt to reassert authority after Brenner had humiliated him in front of his boss.

It was forty minutes before Max Keller reappeared. The twisted smile on his face reflected his crude pleasure at having "put down" the recruit who had dared to challenge him. In case Brenner didn't get the message, he'd rub his nose in it.

"Hope you didn't mind waiting, but I had *important* things to do," he announced grandly. Then he explained what Joey C. Brenner's duties would be.

"You're my helper, see? I don't need one, but Carl thinks I can teach you about special projects. That's what I handle—*special* things."

Things that needed fixing.

Like the arms and legs of people who didn't pay tribute on time. Or the faces of folks who got in Carl Rocca's way. It could be other organs—sometimes whole bodies. Keller would decide what was appropriate in each case.

"I'm the top troubleshooter," he boasted, "and I shoot pretty good."

He grinned as he tapped his shoulder holster. It was going to be a boring day, Brenner guessed accurately. The night was better. They got orders to visit a nightclub that was slow in paying its "premiums."

Kinks.

The name fit the establishment precisely. The main room was a garish chamber all tarted up with too much red rayon satin and polyester plush . . . flash trash at its best-worst. A bar the length of the room faced a long, narrow stage. Behind the bar was a large area crowded with scores of round tables, each circled by cheap, gilded copies of the chairs favored by France's fancy Louis XVI.

If the decor was gaudy and sleazy, it matched the customers. They were a diverse and noisy group: homosexuals, straights, bisexuals, voyeurs, sadomasochists, and two couples from Toronto who thought the whole thing was an interesting change. Almost everyone who wasn't groping, smoking grass, or propositioning somebody was shouting and screaming.

They were responding to the anything-goes show on the stage. There was a female impersonator with great legs, a busty black go-go girl who was five-sixths naked, a blonde stripper with a rhinestone covered G-string and a snake, a husky male strip-tease commando who was emphatically macho, and a pair of swishy and sultry go-go boys. There was also a two-hundred-pound woman in red leather with a whip to complete the sexual circus.

The intensely rhythmic music blasting from four big speakers was recorded and loud. People had to yell over it to be heard by the waiters and waitresses—all in pink hot pants—who circulated with drinks. Everyone seemed very friendly, including a number of customers and two waiters who ogled Joey Brenner with undisguised lust.

Max Keller had been here before. One lipsticked man in his forties winked at him knowingly, and Brenner noticed that Carl Rocca's "top troubleshooter" nodded in discreet response. On the other hand, the large and dramatically attractive woman working the cash register didn't appear to see Keller, let alone know him.

She looked right through him.

He scowled in annoyance.

"Where the hell's Metzger?" he demanded harshly.

"I haven't seen him," she replied.

In a man's voice. The lovely cashier was a transvestite with a gift for numbers.

"How's business?" Keller asked.

"We're dying."

It was a preposterous lie, for the room was packed. Max Keller's features moved in a nasty smile, and then he headed toward the door to the backstage area. As Joey Brenner began to follow, he saw the cashier grab up a telephone.

As the two men entered the backstage section someone erupted from an office and ran. He was a short, slim, and terrified person in his middle years—sprinting to extend them.

"That's him!" Keller yelled.

Joey Brenner bounded down the corridor like a leopard, seized his prey, and slammed him against the door to the dressing room. It flew open under the impact, and Jean Metzger careened back into the brightly lit chamber.

There was a room-length mirror framed by dozens of seventy-five-watt light bulbs. Right below it was a long table covered with assorted lipsticks, rouges, eyebrow pencils, powders, wigs, brushes, and combs. Eight male performers were busy using all this to make themselves look like women. It was a strange sight—unreal.

Metzger tried to flee past them, but there was no escape. Rocca's brutal envoys blocked the only exit. Keller caught Kink's multisexual manager by the wrist, twisted it, and hurled him into the wall with a crash.

The covey of panicky female impersonators began to

shriek. One—in a curly blond wig and boxer shorts—began to sob. Keller ignored them.

"So you're paying off Lamansky now?" he asked.

"He said he'd burn the place if I didn't."

"You must be doin' good," Keller jeered. "Rakin' in enough to pay both of us, huh?"

"I'm not. In fact, I think I'm gonna close."

"No way," Keller told, him and slapped his face hard, four times.

Struggling desperately to break free, the frantic manager made a wild lunge to race past his tormentor. Keller drew a knife, raised it to plunge into Metzger's throat. That was when Joey C. Brenner grabbed the little man and threw him down the long table, sending powder and makeup flying in all directions. A sweet, awful smell—too much and a half—filled the room as Joey Brenner emptied a large jar of blood red makeup over Kink's cringing manager.

"That's what you'll look like *dead*," Brenner threatened. "Not a cent more to Lamansky. Got that?"

Metzger stared at himself in the mirror, began to shudder in uncontrollable horror, and fainted. Brenner shook his head in contempt and started for the door. Knife in hand, Carl Rocca's furious "top troubleshooter" followed him out to the corridor.

"Hey," he said.

Brenner turned.

"Don't *ever* interrupt my play again," Max Keller ordered. "If you do, I'll chop your goddamn head off."

"I might have just saved yours, Max. If you'd aced that punk, this garbage pail would really close—and that would cost Mr. Rocca. I heard guys who do that don't live long, Maxie."

Without waiting for an answer Brenner turned and led the way back to the big crowded room. They were halfway across the chamber when two men blocked their path. It was the detectives Brenner had met in the alley.

"We got a squeal there might be some trouble here," the older plainclothesman said.

It had to be the transvestite cashier who phoned, Brenner computed.

"You know anything about that?" the detective pressed.

"Wasn't me," Brenner replied briskly. "I never squeal."

Detective Sergeant Ira Baker nodded in recognition.

"Clean Joey Brenner. What are you doing in this freak farm?"

"Mr. Keller and I came in for a game of chess," the ex-FBI agent replied nonchalantly as two handsome men kissed at a table a yard away.

"Didn't know you played chess, Max," the detective told Keller. "Did you win?"

"We tied," the mobster replied icily. "We gotta go now."

"See you around, Lieutenant," Brenner said.

"*Sergeant*. Detective Sergeant Ira Baker. Remember that name. I'm going to remember yours."

The hubbub in the room suddenly grew even louder. Customers were cheering and whistling as the blonde stripper on stage began making love to/with her snake. The sounds were deafening as Keller and his "helper" left the nightclub.

"Where you know that cop from, Joey?"

"Met him in an alley near the casino the night you sent those three spitballs to muss my hair. Don't worry, Max. I don't hold grudges."

"I do," Keller answered.

As they walked to the car parked across the street, Mark Kaminski wondered about Detective Sergeant Ira Baker and his habit of turning up in unusual places. Harry Shannon had talked about Patrovita's penetration of the local law-enforcement system.

There was a crooked cop leaking to the mobsters.

Could it be Ira Baker?

26

"*I* want his ass," Lamansky said bitterly.

It was four P.M. the next afternoon. There were a dozen earnest golfers spaced twenty feet apart on the driving range. Ben Lamansky was at one end of the line with eight of his men. Seven were bodyguards. The eighth was Rudy Pasciak, the big bouncer from the gambling joint that Joey Brenner had demolished with the tow truck.

Lamansky pulled back his golf club and swung, topping the ball badly.

He swore.

"I want his stinkin' ass *now*," he announced.

"We're workin' on it," Rudy Pasciak assured. "Don't have a name yet, but he's definitely working for Patrovita."

"Find him," Lamansky ordered as a bodyguard respectfully teed up another ball.

"Real soon."

"Bust his bones, Rudy. All of them. I want it messy, and I want the stiff found. Pound him into jelly so people will get the message. Everybody should know what you get when you kick in Ben Lamansky's door."

"I think he's the same ape who grabbed your car," the bouncer said. "Description fits."

"*Jelly*, Rudy. I want him buried in a jar."

Then he swung again . . . missed the ball completely. The impact of the driver hitting the earth snapped the club's head off.

"Shiiit! I hate this goddamn game!" Lamansky exploded.

The bouncer wanted to ask him why he played it.

He decided not to.

27

A ten-foot-high stone wall surrounded the Patrovita estate, and there were armed guards in the bulletproof guardhouse.

"Joseph Brenner and guest," the undercover agent told them.

After they checked his name and car's license plate numbers against the list on a clipboard, one of the sentries gestured that he could enter. As he guided the Cadillac up the tree-lined driveway, he wondered about the submachine guns he'd glimpsed on a chair in the guardhouse. Standard equipment or recently added insurance against Lamansky raiders?

Now he saw the mansion that he'd read about up ahead.

Four stories high with both passenger *and* freight elevators, seven bedrooms, each with bath; a dining room that seated *thirty-two;* six huge living rooms; library; game and audio-video room; a pair of kitchens with the finest restaurant stoves; indoor swimming pool and gymnasium; and a few rooms for the servants and security men. There was a heated outdoor swimming pool out back. The riding stable behind it had been closed since Patrovita's son moved to Las Vegas where he owned a chain of supermarkets.

Lights glowed in almost every window of the big house, and the sound of music was audible. A score of large, expensive cars was parked near the entrance to the mansion. It looked like a reunion of the Cadillac classes of '85 and '86, with a couple of other luxury cars on the fringes.

When Brenner stopped, a valet hustled to opened Monique Tyler's door to let her out. Brenner slid out from behind the wheel, took a breath of night air, and escorted his blond companion to the front door. The butler who let them in wore a jacket so well cut that Brenner barely noticed the slight bulge under his left armpit.

There was a party inside—in high gear.

A quartet of tuxedo-clad musicians was playing pre-rock music, and eight couples were dancing. Some twenty-six other duos were merrily sipping Chivas Regal Scotch, vintage champagne, and Galliano liqueur; ravaging a long buffet of shrimp, roast beef, caviar, and smoked salmon; and chatting-joking-lying as people do at such events.

Looking around the room, Brenner spotted two familiar faces at once. One was Carl Rocca. The sandy-haired man he was talking to was Swede Swenson. After hearing Special Prosecutor Marvin Baxter ask about him on the video-tape Shannon showed, Kaminski had done some "home-work" on Patrovita and his senior associates—including labor racketeer and hooker-mogul Swenson.

Then Joey Brenner noticed the young girl.

That wasn't hard to do.

She was about twelve, plastered with makeup that was much too sophisticated, and wearing a lace dress with at least forty thousand dollars worth of jewelry.

A professional photographer was reverently taking a picture of her.

Then another . . . and another . . . and three more.

"Who's the starlet?" Brenner jested.

"Don't joke about *her,* Joey," Monique Tyler whispered urgently. "She's Patrovita's granddaughter. Won second prize in the state preteen beauty contest. That's what we're celebrating tonight."

Patrovita had probably put the "fix" in, the undercover agent thought. After all, The Emperor, who'd ordered so many hundreds of deaths, was proud of his reputation as a "good family man." If he could purchase the information to massacre Marcellino and the FBI guards, buying beauty-contest judges would be a snap. He probably didn't even pay them . . . just scared them.

Now Brenner saw Rocca and his "top troubleshooter" walking toward him. Rocca was smiling.

"Glad you could make it, Joey. You, too, Monique."

"Glad you asked me."

"Mr. Patrovita asked you," Rocca corrected in that raspy voice. "He wants to see you."

He didn't say *now.*

He didn't have to.

He turned to lead the way, and Brenner squeezed his companion's arm.

"Be back soon," he promised.

He was right behind Carl Rocca ten seconds later when Max Keller suddenly gestured to the photographer.

"Hey, fella, get a picture of us," he called out loudly as he turned Brenner and Rocca toward the camera.

The undercover agent instantly guessed what was going on. He looked down, started to turn his head. But the flash went off.

"Don't screw around, Max," Rocca scolded. "Mr. P. don't like to be kept waiting."

There was a bodyguard outside the door to the library. When he saw Rocca and Brenner approach, he knocked on the door. They entered a few seconds later.

Paneled walls that once graced a room in a French château.

Hundreds of leather-bound books—probably unread, Brenner guessed.

A marble bust of Julius Caesar atop a sixty-thousand-dollar antique desk.

Expensive silk-covered chairs and a couch.

And windows of bulletproof glass.

The Emperor stood in the middle of the room, an eight-inch Havana in one veined fist and a snifter of amaretto in the other. His face looked thin, his hawk eyes wary. This was a fierce and careful man, the former FBI operative thought—a very shrewd one.

"Lou, this is Joey Brenner," Rocca announced.

"It's an honor to meet you, Mr. Patrovita," Amy Kaminski's husband lied.

The Emperor nodded benignly.

He was used to deference. In fact, he insisted on it.

He scanned and studied the stranger for a dozen seconds before he spoke.

"Mr. Rocca says you might be useful to us."

"I'd like to think so," Brenner replied.

"We like stable people—no ding-a-lings or transients. I hear you don't stay places too long," Patrovita told him.

"If you're not with a strong outfit that can take care of you, moving around is next best. I'd like to settle here."

"He's done some good work for us already," Rocca reminded.

"You kill anybody, Joey?" Patrovita asked.

"Yeah."

"How many?" the ganglord tested.

"Three—for business. I don't kill for fun."

Luigi Patrovita nodded in cautious approval.

"Go back to the party," he ordered. "I gotta talk to Mr. Rocca."

"*Maybe*," The Emperor said a few seconds after Joey Brenner had left the room. "Don't let him in too far . . . too fast. We try him out. If he does right, fine. If he doesn't, use him for something dirty and put him in the lake."

As Patrovita spoke, Max Keller was talking softly to Monique Tyler thirty yards away.

"Found out anything else, baby?"

"I'm working on it."

"Work hard. That's medical advice, kid. If he's rotten and you don't tip us, it'll be lousy for your health," he said with a chuckle.

"Anybody tell you that you're funny, Max?"

He nodded smugly.

"They *lied*," she said. "Hi, Joey. Let's get a drink."

They left a glowering Keller and made their way to the bar. Remembering that remarkable body, she discouraged him from drinking more than two champagnes—urging him to the sumptuous buffet. They left the party at midnight.

"Home, sweet home," she said forty minutes later.

Brenner looked up at Chicago's elegant Palmer House Towers.

"I thought you were broke, Monique."

"I am. Come on up. I'll tell you about it."

Her apartment was on the twenty-seventh floor. There was a wonderful view of the great city from her living room, but they were looking at each other. Sprawled across an armchair, she was wearing a Japanese bathrobe and a cigarette. The cigarette was lit, and the robe was seductively open up to *there*—exposing most of her shapely thighs. His jacket off and tie loosened, the undercover agent faced her from another chair three yards away.

"For five years I was married to a guy who worked for Patrovita. Gerry was good-looking but stupid. He ended up in the gravel pit with no face at all. I suppose they caught him tapping the till once too often, so Patrovita told somebody to tap *him*."

"Why a gravel pit?"

"Not *a* gravel pit. *The* gravel pit. You don't ask questions about Mr. Patrovita's gravel pit—unless you want to end up there. Gerry wouldn't even tell me what they did there. Well, this joint is sort of my pension. It's all I've got."

"No family?"

"A sister in Seattle whom I haven't seen in years. What about you, Joey?"

"I'm from East Germany. When I was nineteen, I got to New York as a sailor on a freighter. Good-bye, Karl Marx."

"You like what you do?"

"Can't beat the money."

"Think this'll be your life's work, Joey?" she asked earnestly.

"Depends on how long I live," he answered with a smile.

Then he rose to his feet and picked up his jacket. He raised the brandy glass and drained the last drops of the Rémy Martin.

Why was he leaving?

Impulsively she moved to him and looked up into his eyes.

"Joey?"

Before he could answer, she kissed him lightly on the lips . . . then more boldly. Now they were both kissing in-

tensely, embracing. As she'd hoped, those powerfully mus-
cled arms were both strong and tender. She pressed against
him. His hand moved slowly...so slowly...down her
spine. Her entire body was tingling with something electrical, magical.

He felt it too. She could tell by the way he kissed her,
long and hard...again and again. His caresses grew more
urgent as the wanting grew. It was happening. Nothing
could stop it now.

But something did.

Suddenly he halted...pulled away.

Just an inch.

It could have been a mile.

They were no longer one—riding the wave.

Why?

Her pride would not let her ask. This kind of man didn't
answer questions. He wasn't like the others who evaded so
easily...lied so well. All her womanly instincts told her
that the moment—*their* moment—had slipped away.

Mark Kaminski looked into her eyes. His blood was still
surging, and his desire was undiminished. Breathing hard,
he wanted to tell her that it wasn't her fault, that it wasn't
anything that she'd said or done. He wanted to tell her about
the woman who wondered and wept in North Carolina, the
woman he loved so totally. Monique Tyler had opened
herself to him, physically and emotionally. She had a right
to know.

But he couldn't explain.

Mark Kaminski was a one-woman man.

He always had been...always would be.

That was his nature.

He never made speeches about it. He didn't feel the least
bit virtuous about it, either. This was his way. He gave

everything to one woman, and he expected everything—
total commitment and connection and content.

But Joey Brenner wouldn't be like that.

All those things were foreign to his life-style and character. They'd be seen as a sign of weakness in his grab-
anything-you-can world. The code there was "Lay 'em and
leave 'em." There were plenty of women, none more
important than another.

It didn't matter whether a gangster was connected with a
Mafia "family" or some other organized crime group.
There was status in sleeping with several women or in
changing your partner to exhibit your "cool" and indepen-
dence and indifference to the restrictions that limited ordinary men. Guys who were "mobbed up"—who were
"connected"—showed off and enjoyed pretty women like
cars or pets. They never got *involved*.

Keller already disturbed him. The incident with the photographer tonight was obviously a move to "check" Joey
Brenner out more thoroughly. The undercover agent couldn't
risk any deviation from the mobster's code, for that would
only make murderous Max Keller even more suspicious.
And there was still the question of Monique Tyler's unpaid
gambling debts. Even if she didn't want to continue spying
on Joey Brenner, the casino lords could squeeze and threat-
en her.

He computed all this in seconds.

Joey Brenner decided to play it safe and "cool."

"See you soon," he announced as he adjusted his tie.

"How about tomorrow afternoon? Come along and help
me pick out a new dress, Joey."

"If I got time," he fenced cautiously. "I'll give you a
buzz."

Maybe he would, he thought as the elevator took him
down a minute later. She could be dangerous, but it might

be worth the risk. She knew many things about the gang and its operations. Perhaps she'd say something more about that gravel pit.

Why would a major mobster worth scores of millions be running a gravel pit?

Just what did the Patrovita organization do out there?

28

There was a magnificent view of Chicago and Lake Michigan from Luigi Patrovita's lavishly furnished office atop the skyscraper. It was a bright, cloudless morning.

He was looking straight out the sleek and slanted picture window that filled half of one wall, but he didn't see the water or the city.

His anger blinded him as he spoke tensely into the phone. He was barely able to control his rage. The Emperor of Life and Death wasn't used to being frustrated.

"This is the Repair Service," he said in barely controlled tones. "We came to fix your water heater, but the *keys* weren't where they were supposed to be."

Key was dope business talk for kilo.

A lot of kilos—$16 million worth of heroin.

"If you'll tell us where the *keys* have been moved," he continued firmly, "we'll come back and take care of the problem."

Then he listened briefly, impatiently . . . frowning.

"Please call us as soon as it's convenient. That water

heater could *blow up* and *hurt* somebody. The company wouldn't want that, and I'm sure you wouldn't like anyone to be *burned,* either. . . . Thanks."

He slammed down the phone.

"A million bucks," he said furiously. "We gave him a goddamn million for word on where Marcellino was, and now he's being cute."

"Maybe he don't know where they're storing the junk," Rocca speculated.

"He can find out. He goddamn better."

Rocca nodded, pretending to agree. He didn't enjoy these situations. Nobody could talk to The Emperor when he got like this.

"Could be he thinks your plan's too dangerous."

Patrovita pounded his fist on the desk.

"*I* do the thinking, and I don't want *no* arguments. I want my cash and my smack."

"It *is* dangerous, you know."

"You're thinking negative, Carl. That's bad. When a guy in our business—with all our guns and money and connections—starts thinking there's something he can't do, he better get out and raise chickens. You like chicken shit, Carl? *I* don't."

Nobody left the Patrovita organization.

Getting out usually meant getting dead.

If The Emperor didn't waste you, his enemies would.

"Hey, I'm not getting out, Lou," Rocca announced with more good cheer than he felt.

"Then get to work. While we're waitin' to hear where the goddamn cops stashed my stuff, go find me that son of a bitch Lamansky. He's gotta have places he goes to regular. A house where his broad lives, a favorite deli, maybe his mother's place."

"I got guys working on that now. We'll have his whole routine soon, and then we hit him."

"By the end of the week, Carl. Four days—no more."

Then Rocca departed. The Emperor lit a Cuban corona, savored a puff, and thought again about the expertly planned and skillfully executed police raid on the heroin house. How had the cops found it? Was it just luck or had someone tipped them?

Was it Lamansky's crowd or somebody else?

Could Luigi Patrovita have a goddamn traitor in his mob?

29

Joey Brenner was starting to get bored.

Trendy high-fashion boutiques had never been his style. He'd been in this one for thirty-five minutes—about thirty-two more than he wanted. It was nearly four P.M., and he had the depressing sense that she wouldn't finish her shopping before five.

She enjoyed it. The prospect of buying a "drop-dead" dress that other women would envy at future parties delighted her. The chance to show off her splendid figure modeling—trying various chic outfits now—to flaunt it to this man who had resisted her—was just as appealing.

She'd let him see that she had a great body too.

Joey Brenner ought to know he wasn't the only one with an exciting shape. It might bring him to his senses, dammit.

"Madam would look *wonderful* in lavender," a hopeful saleslady proposed.

Monique Tyler grinned in anticipation, took the dress, and slipped behind a curtain to try it on in a booth. Half a dozen other women were entering and leaving adjacent booths, eyeing themselves in full-length mirrors and preening.

The salespeople were prattling about a strange variety of colors.

Cerise . . . mauve . . . taupe.

Tints from another galaxy Mark Kaminski had never visited.

After she bought-or-didn't-buy the dress—the eighth that she'd tried—he'd take her out for a drink or two and gently encourage her to speak about her late husband again. Maybe she'd say something—anything more about the gravel pit or some other Patrovita criminal enterprise, mention a name, drop a clue. She wasn't really an evil person, he thought as he waited for her to emerge from the dressing room. He'd try to keep her out of trouble or danger if he could, the undercover agent decided.

In the street outside, three men were hurrying past to their car parked nearby. The biggest of the trio glanced into the boutique—and stopped dead in his tracks.

"It's *him*!" Rudy Pasciak told the other two Lamansky hoodlums.

"You sure?"

"I saw a lot of that bastard—up close—when he was wrecking our joint," the burly bouncer from the demolished gambling spot answered.

"Lucky we were getting some food around the corner," another hoodlum exulted.

"*Un*lucky for Joey inside," Pasciak responded. "Let's do him—slow and mean. Remember what Ben said—*jelly*!"

Inside the shop, Monique Tyler emerged from the booth in a skintight outfit that hid nothing but her birthmarks.

"Think it's right?" she asked.

"For stopping traffic or starting fights. There's not a man alive who won't like that dress."

"And not a woman who won't hate it," she giggled like a mischievous young girl.

"Buy it," Brenner urged as the free-spending mobster. "I'll pay for it."

"You're generous, Joey," she said, beaming.

"No, you're *dead*!" the vengeful bouncer jeered from the doorway. He entered the boutique with the other two thugs at his heels. They raised their fists in menace. One hoodlum wore brass knuckles, and Rudy Pasciak hefted his favorite blackjack.

"Every bone you got," he promised with a nasty smile.

"We're gonna fix your clock," the man with the brass knuckles announced.

"You pimples couldn't fix a toothpick," Brenner said scornfully.

Two of the saleswomen stared at the blackjack and brass knuckles.

"It's a stickup," Brenner told them. "Call your Security."

The boutique employees looked uncertain.

Lamansky's hoodlums attacked. The bouncer was the first to close in, swinging his bone-shattering little club as he approached. Brenner feinted to the left, pulled Rudy Pasciak off-balance, and simultaneously hit him with a hard punch to the nose and a deadly accurate kick in the right knee.

The bouncer stumbled forward, fell facedown into a glass case filled with cultured pearls. The impact shattered the glass top, knocked out three of Rudy Pasciak's teeth, and cascaded a spray of pearls across the floor.

Brenner dodged the metal knuckles; battered the thug wearing them with karate chops to ribs, arm, and temple, and broke his ankle with a kick that made the hoodlum scream. He stopped that when the undercover cop pried off the knuckles, pinched his nose to make him open his mouth, and then crammed the knuckles between his lips.

Sales staff were shrieking. Half-naked women were fleeing

down aisles, jumping behind racks of clothes, and diving into curtained dressing booths. One saleslady was sprawled on the floor—her hair a mess, her chic white ruffled blouse smeared with dirt, and her cool composure a memory.

She had a phone in her hand, terror in her throat.

"Help! Help! We're being robbed! Police! Call the police!" she screamed.

Monique Tyler wasn't shouting. She'd picked up a piece of pipe from a dress rack that had been knocked apart in the melee. She was using it to batter the third thug's head. When he pulled a knife, she pretended to drop the pipe. As he stepped forward the "defenseless" woman swept the metal tube up as hard as she could between his legs.

He screamed even louder than the panicky saleswoman on the phone—once.

Then he joined her on the floor, writhing and gasping. He couldn't even curse. The hurt was too much.

The bouncer was on his feet again. He'd looked ugly before the hand-to-hand combat had begun, and the broken teeth, gashed face, bleeding cuts, and shards of glass in his hair didn't improve his appearance.

"Jelly," he croaked stubbornly.

For a moment Joey Brenner wondered what that meant. Then he decided he'd ask later and broke two of the bouncer's ribs with a power punch instead. An even stronger blow to the solar plexus stopped him dead in his tracks. He rocked on his heels for a few seconds until Monique Tyler swung her pipe again.

"Don't," the ex-FBI agent shouted.

She could kill the bouncer like that.

It was too late to stop her. The pipe crashed into Rudy Pasciak's throat, and he toppled back into a full-length mirror. He had one awful look at the disaster area that was his face before he grabbed for his agonized Adam's apple, slipped on the array of pearls, and fell into the large pane of silvered glass.

Joey Brenner saw it break into nine pieces.

What he didn't see now was the female who'd brought him here.

Suddenly she erupted from one of the booths, clutching her own clothes in one hand and still holding the three-foot piece of pipe in the other. A siren sounded—not far away.

"Let's get the hell out of here before the cops arrive," Brenner urged. "And dump that chunk of iron, will you?"

She wasn't taking any chances. She didn't drop the pipe until they reached the door. As they did, Brenner saw—reflected in the window—the third thug groping under his jacket for a gun. The undercover cop had no desire to be shot or to shoot anyone. He picked up the pipe she'd dropped and threw it.

Accurately.

As his college coach had taught him to hurl a javelin.

It hit the would-be assassin between the eyes like a thunderbolt. He dropped with a fractured skull that would keep him in the hospital for seven weeks.

There was a second siren now.

Nearer.

At that instant she reached out to snatch a jazzy Italian silk scarf from the neck of a plastic dummy. Even in this crisis she couldn't entirely suppress her larcenous impulse. She grinned, and he wanted to spank her.

There wasn't time.

He couldn't afford to be caught by the police here.

"Come on, Monique!" he shouted. "Run!"

She smiled . . . and she ran.

30

The sleek casino under the hotel had been closed for an hour. It was nearly five in the morning, and the gambling establishment was devoid of patrons. Only the Patrovita mob remained.

At one end of the bar The Emperor and Carl Rocca sat on stools—heads together in low-toned conversation. There was always the small possibility that some tricky cops—maybe the feds—had managed to put a "bug" in here to eavesdrop. In light of the extreme sensitivity of what they were discussing, only a suicidal moron would speak above a wary whisper.

Max Keller was behind the bar, pouring himself another double bourbon with ginger ale. Joey Brenner perched on a stool five yards down the bar. The imperial bodyguards—six of them—were seated at tables ten yards away, smoking and sipping beer and searching the room with their eyes.

Even here, even now, they were on maximum alert.

They were always on duty.

They wouldn't relax until the last spade of sod was placed on Ben Lamansky's grave.

Patrovita and Rocca weren't speaking about that deadly competitor tonight. They were talking about The Emperor's rigid determination to recover his property from the police.

"I ain't arguing with you," Rocca said. "Maybe it is possible, but it's going to take a lot of time to figure out and organize."

"*Balls*," Patrovita replied. "We know where it is now. Our pal told me what police station they're using to store it. We get a floor plan, buy an inside man there, and go."

"It won't be that easy, Luigi. This ain't like knockin' over a McDonald's. There's a lot of goddamn firepower in that station all the time. At least forty . . . maybe fifty . . . cops in that building any hour of the day or night. Radios and phones and a teletype. Shotguns and machine guns and bulletproof vests. We can't blast our way into there."

Then Joey Brenner spoke.

"Okay, get the cops out."

"How you gonna do that, wiseass? Give 'em tickets to the circus?" Rocca sneered.

Patrovita was studying the new man thoughtfully.

"A bomb," Brenner said.

"Just blow the place up, huh?" Max Keller mocked.

The undercover agent shook his head.

"What's your idea, Joey?" Rocca asked slowly.

"Scare 'em out. We use bomb threats. When any city department gets one, they gotta evacuate the building. That's in the rules."

"They'll only clear the building if they believe it," Rocca reminded. "They get plenty of phony threats all the time. Why the hell can you make them take this one seriously?"

"More than one," Brenner corrected. "They'll take them seriously all right. I can guarantee it, Mr. Rocca."

"How you gonna do that?" Patrovita questioned.

"By making the cops think somebody's trying to blow up every damn police station in town. We do that with real bombs—a lot of them."

"We give 'em free samples and then we sell the bill of goods, right?" The Emperor tested.

"Exactly, Mr. Patrovita."

The Emperor considered the idea for some fifteen seconds before he nodded.

"I've heard worse ideas, Carl," he said softly. "Looks like your new boy might be useful, after all."

31

Built in 1957, it was one of the newer police stations in the city. It was always busy here in the Ninth. The stream of uniformed cops flowing in and out was nothing special. This was an ordinary afternoon.

There were civilians entering and leaving too. One of them was wearing a uniform—the coveralls and cheery smile of the Dandy Food Corporation. He parked the delivery van, took a rack of candy and snacks from the back, and carried his inventory through the front door.

"Hey! Where you goin'?" the cop at the complaint desk inside challenged as he sauntered past.

"Dandy. I'm the route man. Here to fill your machines. It's Wednesday, right?"

"Where's Bobby?"

Another big grin.

All these guys were heavy on the charm, the cop thought. Those fat smiles were probably as automatic as the machines the route men serviced.

"*Where's Bobby?* That's what our boss would like to know. Say, you guys bigger on potato or corn chips? The boys over at the Sixth don't even touch the corn," the delivery man reported briskly.

He was playing it fast and casual—just right. He wasn't overdoing it. He'd had plenty of experience at this game, with years of success as a confidence man, scam artist, and swindler. Only three arrests. Just a single conviction. Easy time—twenty-eight months.

"If you want my opinion on the chips," he continued, "I'd say—"

But he didn't.

The desk phone rang, and the policeman on duty lifted it immediately. As he did so, he waved to the route man to stop chattering and get on with his business. Busy speaking on the telephone to another Patrovita operative who had timed the call carefully, the cop ignored the coveralled stranger with the tray of snacks.

"Junk food for my junk," Patrovita had joked. "Not a bad deal."

The man in the Dandy Foods uniform didn't waste a minute or a step. He didn't have to. He'd studied the floor plan that Carl Rocca had bought from a greedy clerk in the Building Department, and he knew every corridor and room, every stairway and steam pipe.

He walked directly to the alcove marked CANTEEN.

There were the beverage and food machines, exactly as indicated on the chart.

Then he took out the keys that Rocca had provided, and he carried out the instructions.

Easy as pie, he thought as he made his way back to the front of the station house. The cop at the desk was busy fielding another call.

"Ninth District, Officer Moore," he singsonged, and nodded farewell to the counterfeit route man.

"Have a good day," the cheery criminal called out as he waved back.

He was humming as he climbed behind the wheel of the delivery van. It was a pleasure to work with a solidly "pro" outfit such as The Emperor's. They had the floor plan, the delivery schedule, and the access to the genuine driver, who didn't want his kid brother in the pen at Joliet to lose an eye.

The driver started the motor, cruised down to the corner, and stopped for a red light. Chicago had twenty-five police districts, each with a station house. He wondered why Rocca had chosen the Ninth for this very special delivery.

The light was changing. He glanced at his watch, saw what time it was, and thought about the twenty-five hundred dollars he'd receive. There would be an airline ticket to Mexico in the envelope with it. It would be wiser to go away for a month in case somebody remembered the "new" route man's face.

He looked in the rearview mirror now.

First he head the blast. Then a column of smoke poured from the station house, and a couple of dazed men in uniform tottered out.

"Have a *very* good day," he whispered triumphantly.

Then he stepped on the gas to get away from this neighborhood as quickly as legally possible.

Someone might recall the van or its license plates.

Why stick around to find out?

32

A lot of people arrived at the bomb-shaken Ninth in the next twenty minutes.

Firemen with their axes and hoses to extinguish any flames.

Ambulance teams with litters, oxygen, and assorted medical gear.

Emergency service crews.

A bomb-squad unit in their armored truck and strange safety suits.

A battle-ready Special Weapons and Tactics squad, a SWAT unit carrying heavy hardware and loaded for bear.

Eight patrol cars from the Ninth that heard about the explosion on the police radio.

A local priest who thought someone might require last rites.

Two neighborhood lawyers. One was confident that the "terrible incident" had been caused by the "negligence of the gas company" and was ready to sue the shorts off it. Less ambitious, the other attorney was prepared to settle his client's claim against the city as soon as he got a client.

A "meat wagon" and medical examiner, both belonging to the coroner's office and passing nearby when word of the blast spewed from their radio.

A quartet of forensic and laboratory technicians from police headquarters, frowning as each of them collected, bagged, and tagged evidence. Their balding and bespectacled supervisor—lanky Leonard Hunt—was speaking earnestly with the special prosecutor assigned to nail Luigi Patrovita. It was the same hard-boiled crime buster who had handled the brutality charges against Mark Kaminski—rough and righteous Marvin Baxter.

"Yes, it *could* be an organized crime deal," forensic specialist Hunt agreed.

"That's why I'm here," Baxter told him. "I'll take anything that could give me a handle on somebody who's mobbed up . . . who could tell us how to rattle The Emperor's cage. A hood facing time inside can get very chatty if we squeeze him."

"It's a long shot, Marv."

Baxter turned to face graying Harry Shannon, the avenging father who had launched Mark Kaminski as a human missile against the Patrovita organization.

"Longer than that," Baxter admitted frankly, "but a good prosecutor doesn't miss a chance. What brings you into this mess, Harry? Some federal business involved?"

"The Bureau catches heat whenever a bomb goes off," the FBI agent said. "Bombs mean terrorism, and that's our turf."

"Have you had word about terrorists blasting police stations?" Baxter wondered.

"There are rumors. Who but crazy terrorists would bomb a police station?" Shannon asked as he ran a finger over a gritty smear on a broken wall.

"You find something?"

"Feels like black powder. Pretty crude explosive. Not what a pro would use to wreck a building."

Hunt's technicians moved in to take samples, and Shannon and Baxter retreated to get out of their way.

"How's it going, Harry?" Baxter asked sympathetically.

"It still hurts—but I'll live. Any progress on your Patrovita case?"

Baxter shrugged.

"We're working on a new angle. And if that doesn't pay off, we try another. I'm going to get that hoodlum. He's going to run out of tricks before I run out of patience," the prosecutor vowed.

"They took me off the case, you know," Shannon said angrily, "but I'm like you. I'm not giving up on this one."

"Don't worry, Harry. We'll get Patrovita sooner or later."

"Later's not good enough. I'm not waiting."

The by-the-book district attorney understood and looked uneasy.

"I hope you're not saying what I think," he told the bitter father. "We're doing all we can."

"So am I."

"Please, you could get into a lot of trouble. Let us handle it. We're all after the same thing—justice."

"I'll settle for Patrovita's ashes myself," Harry Shannon announced grimly.

Then he turned and headed for the street.

There could be no doubt about it, the special prosecutor thought.

Indifferent to the risk of hurting some covert official operation against Patrovita's far-flung "family," he was attacking on his own.

Marvin Baxter wasn't going to tell the FBI about the grieving father's private crusade, but if the Bureau found out, it might end Harry Shannon's career.

And if Patrovita found out, he'd end Harry Shannon.

The Emperor didn't take chances, Baxter reflected as he started back to where the lab technicians were working.

He never had, and he certainly wasn't likely to start now.

It would be earnest, honest Harry Shannon who'd be reduced to ashes.

One cop *couldn't* take on the rich and ruthless Patrovita organization. There wasn't a single person in the state—in the country—who could do that. No sane person would dare to try it. Even a Dirty Harry supercop wouldn't attempt that.

Baxter did not take Joseph Clean Brenner into consideration.

He hadn't heard of him—*yet*.

33

Max Keller was a terrible person in many ways, but there were some things that he was good at.

Protecting his turf was one of them—as a lot of people had learned the hard way.

Holding a grudge was another.

Letting go of enmity was as foreign to him as paying taxes or respecting the Ten Commandments, of which he only remembered two, anyway.

He'd hated Joey Brenner from the moment they'd met.

For daring to muscle in on his job, for hurting his body and pride in front of Rocca, for easily kicking the crap out of his handpicked trio in the alley, for interfering in the sewer that was Kink's, for winning the favors of the beautiful blonde Keller had sent against him.

Though he had no proof, Keller was infuriated by the conviction that the son of a bitch had seduced the dazzling woman whom Keller had ordered to seduce *him*. It was maddening to think that the lovely face and shapely body that had once been Keller's property—briefly—was not pleasing this cocky punk who had just breezed into town.

That added to his outrage. So did the fact that Patrovita had accepted this wise guy's scheme for recovering the dope and money. Monique Tyler would suffer after Keller had destroyed Brenner. That came first, and that was why Keller was in the photoduplicating store now.

"You said fifty?" the denim-clad young clerk asked.

Keller nodded, and the machine began to spit out copies of the picture of Rocca, Brenner, and Keller taken at the Patrovita mansion. Brenner's head was circled on the glossy print that was being duplicated.

That was all Max Keller wanted these days.

Brenner's head.

It was even more important than Lamansky's—for the moment. Both men would soon be dead, of course. Keller hoped that he'd have the great pleasure of slaying them himself. He'd spent hours thinking of unusual and painful ways to do it. Broken glass in food, acid in eye-drops or a cocktail, a blowtorch "massage" or slow crushing while conscious in a car compactor were some of his first ideas. He knew that he'd probably have to settle for a shotgun blast in the face, but he could dream, couldn't he?

"Okay, here's your fifty," the clerk said.

He put the original and the copies in a fat envelope and accepted Keller's twenty-dollar bill.

Now it was just a matter of distributing the copies to the right people in Miami, New Orleans, Detroit, L.A., Boston, Cleveland, Vegas, and Washington. The Emperor had somebody on the pad who had connections inside the Department of Justice itself. Max Keller didn't know his identity. Only Patrovita and Rocca shared that secret. Whoever he was, he could be invaluable in finding out who the creep who said he was Joey Brenner from Miami *really* was.

If he was a gun named Joey Brenner, Keller would have some way to kill him "accidentally" on some job. If he was a liar, Keller would ask Carl Rocca to let him finish the bastard off in one of the grisly ways that he'd imagined.

The nastier the better.

People had to be reminded about the facts of life every once in a while.

If you screwed around with the Patrovita organization, you died dirty.

That was one of The Emperor's own Ten Commandments.

Hell, it was all of them.

34

*I*t was time to report again.

Carefully.

The goddamn problem was that you couldn't be sure that you were being careful *enough*.

He certainly couldn't call from his apartment or any phone in the gambling casino or the hotel above it. Even the telephone booths in the area weren't entirely safe. Between the local and state police and the whole grab bag of federal agencies—the Bureau; Internal Revenue; CIA; Army, Navy, and Air Force intelligence outfits; and who knew what else—there was a ton of wiretapping going on.

Well, a call inside the city was at least safe from one other eavesdropping organization, Mark Kaminski thought as he made his choice. With intercity calls—especially longer distance ones—going by microwave you could be taped by some sophisticated Soviet spy *apparat* routinely sweeping the airwaves with advanced "ears" for intelligence information.

He found the movie theater showing the new Disney nature picture, bought a ticket, and called from the booth downstairs beside the men's toilet. It was less likely that anyone would tap a phone in a "house" showing a picture that would pull a kid audience, he reasoned. Still possible— and Patrovita had that informer somewhere in the law-enforcement system.

The phone rang twice.

Then he heard Shannon speak.

The voice was the same, but the words were different.

Instead of "Please leave your message," the tape now asked callers to "Please leave a *brief* message and include your *phone number*." Those code words signaled that Harry Shannon was calling an emergency meeting at five in the afternoon.

Shannon had chosen a shabby old part of the city for his "safe house." It wasn't a house at all, just a small apartment in a tired old building that had one outer wall blackened by a fire. A few years ago there had been some people in this decaying neighborhood who'd set blazes for one reason or another. Landlords had hired professional "torches" to ignite aged tenements for the insurance, and junkies and derelicts and an assortment of teen hooligans had lit their own conflagrations. Half of the buildings across the street from the "safe" studio had gone up in smoke.

When he heard the knock, Harry Shannon drew his pistol.

Only Kaminski knew the address, but Shannon wasn't taking any chances.

"Who is it?" he asked, pointing the gun at the door.

"Me," Mark Kaminski's familiar voice replied.

Shannon opened the door, let him in, and immediately closed and chained it shut again.

"I've only got a few minutes."

"That's all I need. You did too good a job on Lamansky," the graying FBI agent announced. "He has you marked.

They know you're Joey Brenner, and they know what you look like. He's put fifty grand on your head."

"Only fifty?"

"It's no joke, Mark. You either have to cut and run, or look over your shoulder all the time." .

"Those cheap bastards came close the other day."

Shannon opened two bottles of beer and handed one to his visitor. They each downed a swallow.

"Word is they just ran into you," the older man reported.

"Ran in and crawled out."

"You were damn lucky, Mark. They'd been in court nearby earlier, so they weren't carrying pieces."

Now Shannon took another pull at the bottle, and Kaminski noticed the trio of empties on the floor. He couldn't help thinking about his wife. Was her drinking under control or worse?

Another concern flashed through his mind.

How much alcohol was bitter Harry Shannon downing?

If he lost control, it could cost both the graying FBI agent and Kaminski their lives.

"I wondered why they didn't pull guns," the "dead" sheriff said. "They're going to need them when Patrovita's hoods come blasting. They're figuring where to hit Lamansky right now."

Shannon wandered to the window, looked down to make sure that no one was watching the building, and shrugged.

"I don't give a shit if gangsters kill gangsters—not anymore," he announced. "All I care about is Patrovita in that icebox at the Cook County morgue."

"Patrovita's kind of busy right now. He's getting ready to grab back his heroin and cash from the local cops. Those bombs in the three station houses this week are part of his plan,'' Kaminski said, and explained what The Emperor meant to do.

"That's a pretty good scheme."

"Glad you like it."

"*Your* idea?" Shannon asked.

"Joey Brenner's no dummy. He knows how to impress the boss."

Shannon looked worried.

"Bombs in police stations? You're *crazy!*" he erupted.

"Just a little. The bombs are little too . . . not big enough to *kill* anybody. You want to stop it?"

Shannon considered the situation and shook his head.

"Might be too risky for you," he said. "If something goes wrong, they'll figure the new guy for the leak. Let 'em take it all. I don't like it, but it's your ticket in."

"That was the idea."

"You found out anything about who Patrovita's spy is?"

"Not yet, Harry. There's something I'd like you to find out for me. Would you check out a city detective named Baker? Sergeant Ira Baker seems to show up in the wrong places at the right times."

"Baker? Think he's Patrovita's man?"

"Who the hell knows? It could be a woman . . . or a couple of people. I've got to split now," Kaminski said, and put down the bottle.

Then he eyed the one in Harry Shannon's hand.

The FBI agent noticed it.

"No, Mark. And those empties on the floor are yesterday's. I'm not much of a housekeeper, but I'm not on the sauce, either."

It would be nice to be sure, Kaminski thought as he left.

Nice but impossible.

35

Business was booming.

The underground casino was crowded with well-dressed couples. Enjoying the free drinks and phony glamour, the affluent patrons chatted and laughed as they lost and won and lost again.

Thousands of dollars.

It didn't appear to bother them.

They were paying for the thrills and the right to show off, Joey Brenner realized. They were showing off their wealth, their stylish clothes, and their "cool." Shrinks who talked solemnly about gamblers' "death wishes" were missing a key point. For a lot of these bored rich, this was recreation. The fact that big-league criminals ran it only added spice to the expensive diversion.

Monique Tyler picked up her chips from the baccarat table, took a seat on a stool near the end of the bar, and looked around for the man with the kind eyes and magnificent body. Where the hell was Joey? Men didn't usually keep the dazzling blonde waiting. Annoyed, she nodded to the curly-haired bartender for her "usual."

"Thanks, Jimmy," she said when he delivered it twenty seconds later.

"Pleasure," he responded.

"That's what I'd like," Max Keller said suddenly from beside her.

"Read a comic strip," she suggested, and sipped her drink.

"I'm talking me and you."

"Let's keep this business, Max. I don't wanna hurt your feelings," she told him, "but the only way you'll be lying down near me is if we're hit by the same taxi."

Goddammit, she was sleeping with Brenner.

She had to be to talk like this.

Maybe the bitch needed a lesson.

He put his right hand at the base of her neck, clamped his fist like a vise, and squeezed hard to hurt her.

He did.

The agony showed in her face. She tried to control her voice, but the pain prevailed. Tears trickling from her eyes, she yelped helplessly.

"Like it, baby?" Keller taunted. "I do."

"Then be my guest," Joey Brenner invited.

Both his massive hands were forcing down on the back of the sadist's own neck now—applying enormous pressure. The superbly fit ex-FBI man increased it steadily. Crippled with paralyzing pain, Keller's arms dropped limply to his sides.

His eyes were wide and wet.

His neck veins bulged as he struggled not to scream.

Gasping, he lost control and his knees buckled. Brenner wasn't ready to let him off the hook yet. He held Keller off the floor and continued the relentless hurting.

"You look sick, Max," he finally said. "Go home and take a couple of Tylenol capsules."

Then he let go and Keller tottered back, barely able to stand. He reeled away, turned, and surrendered to a tidal wave of fury. Spinning around to face his enemy, Keller reached under his jacket for his gun.

He was looking into the muzzle of Brenner's Beretta.

"What kind of box, Max? Pine or walnut?"

The reference to coffins made Keller freeze. Panting and glaring in frustration, he barely managed to control his rage. The pain was still awful when he limped away.

"I'm impressed," Monique Tyler said.

"I'm hungry," Brenner replied.

She picked up her glass, and they made their way to a table to order dinner.

"I don't understand you, Joey," she said abruptly. "Why are you late? You want to see me or not?"

"I don't want you to see those goons who jumped me in the dress store," he answered. "They'll be back—with guns."

"The hell with guns. I'm talking about you. What is it? You married or something?"

He nodded slowly.

"Where is she?"

"A long way from here," he replied truthfully. "Listen, Monique, I like you a lot. That's why I bought you the dress. I want to be friends."

"Friends? You son of a bitch!"

She grabbed her coat that had been draped over an adjacent chair and put it on. It didn't surprise Brenner that she was angry and wanted to leave.

What she did next did surprise him.

Reaching inside the coat, she began to strip off the dress that he'd bought her.

"If I want to make friends, mister, I'll go to summer camp!" she said loudly.

People turned at the noise.

Then they gaped.

She whipped out the dress and jammed it into Brenner's hands.

"Keep it, *friend*!"

She was standing there with the coat half open, revealing a black garter belt, black mesh nylons, mini black panties, a hint of a brassiere, and a lot of skin.

She picked up her cigarette, took a final puff, and dropped it into Brenner's drink.

"So long, *friend*!" she shouted.

Half the people in the big room stared as she swivel-hipped out, the coat flapping open as she moved.

Brenner looked at the dress for a few seconds.

Maybe it was for the best.

She was as lovely as she was dangerous, and he was a lonely man a long way from home.

So it was over.

Okay, he'd get no more information or help from Monique Tyler.

He was all alone again in the impossible war.

There was but one thing to do now, and he did it.

He flagged down the waiter and ordered a fresh drink.

36

*A*t 9:05 the next morning, the phone rang in Brenner's flat.

At 9:25 he hurried from the building and walked swiftly to the dark green Buick sedan at the curb. Max Keller was behind the wheel, and one of the hoodlums who'd tried to batter the ex-F.B.I. man that night in the alley sat behind him.

"This is Dingo," Keller said as Joey Brenner entered the car.

"We've met. Feeling any better?"

The thug didn't answer. Keller shoved the sedan into gear and moved it out into the flowing traffic.

"What's the emergency, Max?" Brenner asked.

"Don't you work good on short notice?"

"Everybody works better if they know what the hell's going down."

"Lamansky's goin' down. We're hitting The Snake in half an hour. He's saying his prayers right now," Keller announced with a nasty chuckle.

At 9:50 Keller stopped the Buick on a quiet street in a residential area on the North Side.

"Get ready," he said, and pointed to a large building half way up the next block. Joey Brenner looked at the stained glass windows . . . saw a big six-pointed Star of David. It was a synagogue.

"I told you he was prayin'." Keller chuckled. "Poor ol' Benny. He ain't religious at all. Comes once a year on the anniversary of his mama's dying. Well, he'll be joining her real soon."

The chips were down.

What the undercover agent had hoped would never happen was only minutes away.

They expected him to help kill somebody.

Joey Brenner wouldn't mind blasting an enemy in a sneak attack, but gunning down someone in an ambush was against Mark Kaminski's principles and instincts.

Was there any way out?

"It's a shrewd plan, Max," he complimented, "but I always thought churches were out of bounds. Even those trigger-happy Latino coke mobs in Florida wouldn't hit a guy in a church."

"Not *in* the church. When he comes *out*." Keller chuckled. "We'll tail him a few blocks before we blow his Hebrew head off. Son of a bitch won't know what hit him."

It would be a surprise, all right.

Lamansky wouldn't expect an attack here.

Brenner studied the block near the synagogue, saw a single large limousine. There wasn't the usual second car crammed with bodyguards. Feeling safe going to a house of worship, Ben Lamansky was traveling with a minimum security force.

"I don't like it much," Brenner fenced.

"Don't *like* it. *Do* it . . . here he comes."

A score of worshipers trickled from the synagogue. Ben Lamansky emerged in the middle of them with two bodyguards. Dressed in a dignified dark gray suit, he looked thoughtful as he silently walked to his maroon Cadillac—a replacement for the one Brenner had ruined. There was a driver waiting at the wheel.

"*Four* of them," Joey Brenner pointed out. "They've probably got a Uzi in the car. We should have more people with us."

He was right, but Keller ignored his reasoning.

"Scared, Joey?" he mocked.

Before Brenner could answer, the Lamansky car pulled away, and Keller fed gasoline to the Buick. The hunt was on. Nothing could stop it now.

They cruised down the street thirty yards behind the Cadillac. Brenner heard a metallic click behind him and looked in the mirror. In the rear seat Dingo was checking out a high-powered rifle.

"He's got explosive ammo," Keller announced. "When we get out of heavy traffic and he has a clear shot, he'll blow the gas tank. We're gonna fry Mrs. Lamansky's little boy."

"He'll bail out."

"That's when you and I blast him, Joey. Relax, I got it all figured."

The limousine turned up a street with light traffic.

"Any second now, Dingo," Keller said as he moved the Buick closer.

As it drew nearer, the Cadillac driver spotted it in his side-view mirror.

"Somebody's coming up fast, Ben," he warned.

Lamansky peered out the rear window and immediately guessed what was happening.

"Trouble," he said. "Lose them."

His driver stepped on the gas. One bodyguard pulled a .357 Magnum as the other lifted a submachine gun from the floor. Joey Brenner had been right. It was a Uzi.

"Okay, Dingo," Keller said.

The rifleman behind him rolled down his window, raised the high-powered weapon, and leaned out to shoot. He took aim . . . fired twice.

He didn't miss.

He didn't blow up the gas tank, either.

Keller cursed as he saw the bullets glance off the Caddy.

"You should have brought a bazooka," Brenner told them. "That limo's armored."

Dingo scored two more hits—which did nothing.

"I'm going run that goddamn tank off the road," he swore.

"How?" Brenner asked. "He's got a ton of weight on us, and their wheelman looks pretty good."

"He won't when you put a slug in his teeth."

The rifleman fired another shot that disfigured, but didn't penetrate, the limousine's rear window. Now the Lamansky bodyguard who had the Uzi was halfway out a window, pouring short bursts from the 9-millimeter weapon.

Keller zigzagged the Buick. The bastard was a skillful driver, the undercover cop thought. Now Dingo had put down the rifle and was firing back with a semiautomatic M16. Both vehicles moved faster and faster, barreling through traffic lights as if they didn't exist.

Keller jammed the gas pedal to the floor, cursed as a burst from the Uzi sliced a gash in the Buick's hood. He swung the green sedan back and forth, screaming obscenities in a steady stream.

Closer and closer.

Brenner tensed, wondering whether Keller had gone crazy and was going to ram the bigger vehicle.

At that moment a milk company's refrigerated tank truck moved out of a side street—right into the murderous cross fire. The stunned driver took one look, slammed on his brakes, and dropped to the floor. Two seconds later the machine guns ripped fifty holes in the thin-skinned tank, and dozens of jets of milk squirted into the air in all directions.

The gangsters' cars raced on.

Only a few yards separated them now.

Keller suddenly saw his chance. He'd let Lamansky's guns wipe out the man he hated most. There was no way Rocca could blame Max Keller if The Snake's bodyguards killed Brenner in this wild melee.

Keller crept the Buick up near the rear of the Cadillac. Exactly as he'd hoped, a window rolled down, and the Uzi hammered at the nearest target—Joey Brenner. Bullets demolished the window beside Brenner, chewed the dashboard to shreds.

The next burst from the Uzi would have him.

It never came.

Brenner shot the machine gunner between the eyes. The Uzi dropped to the street as the corpse fell back into the limo.

Then Brenner turned to point his Beretta at Keller.

"Want me to drive?" he said.

Keller let the Buick fall back. The armored limousine began to widen the gap. Lamansky was escaping.

The hoodlum beside the Cadillac driver leaned out to get off another round. Instead he caught three. Dingo's M16 tore holes in his face, and he reeled back inside, gushing blood. As his life poured out, he thrashed blindly like the dying animal he was.

That was when Lamansky's driver lost control.

Not of his car.

Of his mind.

Hysterical, he jerked the big limousine in a desperate right turn to escape the death raining from the Buick. The green sedan followed relentlessly. He could see it in his mirror.

The body beside him was still twitching . . . convulsing.

Blood sheeted half the windshield.

And bullets from the hunters crashed against the rear window, pounding insistently like the fist of a homicidal giant.

The bulletproof glass couldn't take much more.

Parked trailer trucks lined both sides of the block. He had to find an opening . . . a way out. Now he saw a gap, and he rammed the Cadillac into it without thinking.

He couldn't calculate anymore.

All he could do was flee—as fast as the big machine would go.

He was so frightened that he could hardly see. He barely noticed that he wasn't on a street anymore. Lamansky was shouting something, but it was hard to make it out.

There were metal columns on either side . . . stacks of crates. He couldn't pay attention to them. The dying man was still thrashing, bumping into the driver again and again. The panicky wheelman frantically pushed the terrible creature away, as if death were some contagious disease he'd catch.

There was daylight ahead.

Suddenly the driver realized where he was.

The Cadillac was racing at ninety miles an hour down a *pier*.

It was not escape that lay ahead.

It was the icy embrace of Lake Michigan.

"Look out!" Lamansky yelled desperately.

It was too late. The heavy limousine hurtled off the end of

the pier and hit the water like a boulder. The armored Cadillac bucked, turned on its side, and lay there for a few seconds.

Ben Lamansky clawed for the door controls to get out. But the great lake came in before he could escape. Numbing cold water poured through the Cadillac's open windows, forcing out the air that might have given him time to break free.

Then the massive car and the two terrified men in it slid beneath the surface and died. Watching from the battered Buick near the end of the pier, Joey Brenner, Keller, and Dingo saw the last air bubble rise. Now the waters were smooth again.

Keller turned the green sedan around and drove away, careful not to exceed the speed limit. He didn't speak until the Buick was half a mile from the pier.

"My plan wasn't so bad, after all," he boasted.

"It was great, Max," Dingo agreed enthusiastically. He went on praising his boss for half a minute before Keller abruptly flicked on the police radio.

The first call was about an auto accident on Division.

The second dealt with discovery of a bomb in the headquarters of the Third District.

Now the undercover cop understood why he'd been assigned to the hit team . . . and why more of Patrovita's forces hadn't been sent to help.

The Third was where the heroin and money were cached.

He'd been chosen for the death squad to prove himself, because they still didn't trust him fully. The other gunmen who should have been on the hit team were busy at the police station.

Using Joey Brenner's plan, they were carrying out the biggest robbery in North American history—right now.

37

*I*t had begun thirty-one minutes earlier.

There were nine men and a van in a garage half a mile from the station house that was headquarters for the Third District. Bold, black lettering on the side of the vehicle identified it: CHICAGO POLICE DEPT.—BOMB DISPOSAL UNIT.

Eight of the men were inside the van. It was a real police vehicle. Rocca had paid a corrupt sergeant ten thousand dollars to let it be stolen shortly before dawn . . . and to misdirect the report of the theft. Special "safety" suits and visors and other bomb-handling gear hung securely on double-catch hooks along the inner walls. There was a portable blast-absorbing bomb-disposal chamber. A few feet away was a well-equipped communications center with three radiophones.

The eight men wore police uniforms. These were authentic garb of the Chicago Police Department. Though the uniforms were real, these cops were not. Not one of them was actually a member of the Chicago or any other police department. They were criminals who worked for The Emperor, handpicked for their ability to speak and act like cops.

No unusual accents or facial features.

Nothing that might be questioned or remembered.

Two blocks away, another man in a jumpsuit was waiting in a manhole. He wore a belt loaded with phone company tools, and he stood beside a main telephone cable that he'd scraped open. He'd bridged two sets of wires and had his hand on a switch. His other hand held a walkie-talkie.

"Ready?" he asked into a short-range radio.

"Ready," a fake policeman holding a walkie-talkie replied from the garage.

The criminal in the manhole closed the switch. A moment later a counterfeit cop at the communications console in the van began to dial. The phone rang three times before it was answered.

"Third District, Officer Lopez."

"This is the People's Brigade. You got a bomb in the building. It goes off in twenty-two minutes."

The fake policeman at the console hung up a second before he pressed a switch at the bottom of the control panel. A loud set-your-teeth-on-edge wave of electronic static surged from the loudspeaker above the console.

"Everything's jammed," he said. "Let's roll."

In the police station, Officer Lopez took the howling phone from his ear.

"*Shit,*" he complained in direct violation of orders against foul language. Then he sprinted to the captain's office to report.

"Now *we've* got the bomb! They phoned in—People's Brigade. It's gonna blow in twenty-two minutes."

"Call the bomb squad," Captain Milton Jacobs replied crisply, "and clear the building. Everybody out—on the double."

Jacobs pointed to the red alarm switch on the wall. Lopez

pulled it, and before he was out of the captain's office, the klaxon was roaring. Manny Lopez hurried back to his desk to dial the bomb squad. He got the communications console in the stolen van.

"Bomb Disposal. . . . Where? . . . Okay, evacuate the building and take up perimeter positions three hundred feet away. Nobody gets nearer. . . . Sure, we're on our way."

The counterfeit policemen studied the station house floor plan once more and went over their plan and procedures again.

Calmly . . . carefully . . . with no rush.

They shouldn't arrive for another eight or nine minutes, anyway.

When they neared the station house, they saw how efficient Captain Jacobs and the men of the Third were. The perimeter was in place, and Jacobs informed them that the building was empty.

"You're lucky," a fake cop in an armored safety suit told him. "They didn't phone ahead at the other headquarters. I guess this bomb must be a lot bigger. Hell, there could be a couple."

Scores of curious civilians and some forty police officers watched as the impostors hauled out their bomb chamber and carried it into the building. Once inside, three of them raced through the station house, double-checking that there was no one else in the headquarters. One—with walkie-talkie—watched the front door.

The others hurried to the Property and Evidence Vault. They took plastic explosives from the bomb chamber and began packing charges into place on the door expertly. Two of them were top-notch safecrackers who'd once been skilled demolition men in the army.

"Piece of cake," one said.

Some ninety seconds after he spoke, they blew the door off its hinges. Moments after it crashed to the floor, they began carrying out Luigi Patrovita's property and stacking it inside the bomb chamber.

It all went quickly and neatly.

Just the way they had rehearsed it—four times.

It wasn't exactly military precision, but it was close enough.

The supervisor who had ordered the real cops to evacuate and keep everyone away stood watching, checking his watch regularly. They had scheduled this phase for three minutes—no more.

"You got fifty seconds," he warned.

They finished with nineteen seconds to spare. They shut and bolted the bomb chamber, adjusted their blast visors again, and hauled their heavy and precious cargo up to the street.

"All clear?" Captain Jacobs called out over his bullhorn.

The leader of the criminals waved his men on to their van. He followed behind them until he reached Jacobs.

"What's up? Can we go back?"

"Not till we get the van out of here. Those bastards hid two—just the way I figured. Same as they did last month in L.A., dammit. We detonated one, and we're taking the other in the chamber."

"L.A.?" Jacobs asked.

"The goddamn People's Brigade. Killed three cops. You must have read about it."

The captain nodded—very sincerely.

"Give us five or six minutes to clear the area," the impostor said, "and then you can go back. We've called for a cleanup crew to help you. Sorry we had to detonate the first one."

Better you than us, the captain thought.

He didn't say that. Instead he thanked the bomb disposal unit and watched the van roll out of sight.

Word of the sensational robbery didn't reach the media until ten minutes after one.

That was nearly three hours before Max Keller got the phone call from Miami.

38

Midnight.
   Millions of Chicagoans were asleep.

Next week some of them would be sleeping in the rectangular wooden-and-metal containers in this big dimly lit room.

Okay, not *these*—but ones exactly like them.

These coffins were display models on exhibit in the Gibson Funeral Home, a medium-priced establishment that had been tactfully, tastefully, and profitably serving Chicago's bereaved for some half a century.

There were three men in the room.

Luigi Patrovita stood in the middle of the chamber, dominating it as an emperor should.

Patrovita was under an overhead lamp. Lurking outside the circle of light was another person—someone cautious who preferred the shadows.

On guard near the door lounged Max Keller, jacket unbuttoned in case he had to get to his weapon quickly. There was no reason to expect trouble, but Keller always did. He believed the worst about everyone and every situation. He was usually right.

"Tell him, Max," The Emperor ordered.

"There's this guy showed up a coupla weeks ago. Came to Mr. Rocca at the casino for a job. He didn't look right to me, but Mr. Rocca decided to give him a try."

"He said he was Joseph C. Brenner from Miami," Patrovita announced.

"I remember checking him out for you," the man in the shadows said.

"Not good enough."

"I did the usual thing—the NCIC computer. I gave you the printout with his record."

"That was Joey Brenner's record. Tell him about your phone call this afternoon, Max," Patrovita ordered.

"I decided to double-check myself. Just a hunch," Keller said. "So I had a guy take a picture of him and sent copies to a lot of people. The right people in different places. Guys we done business with for years."

"What's the point of all this?" the voice in the darkness questioned.

"Shut up and listen," Patrovita said. "For a million bucks you listen."

"Well, I got a phone call from a buy in Miami this afternoon. He showed the picture to a detective down there—a cop he pays regular. That detective *knows* Joey Brenner. Busted him twice a coupla years ago. He says Joey Brenner's down in Panama."

"*What?*" the cultured voice asked.

"I'll spell it out," Patrovita declared contemptuously. "This guy you checked out so fine and federal *ain't* Joey Brenner. He's a *phony*."

"Who is he?"

"I'm gonna find out—before I bury him. You're gonna help, pal," The Emperor announced.

"Get me his prints and I'll check them in Washington. That ought to do it."

"Unless somebody's screwing around with the FBI print files. Is that possible?"

"I don't know."

"What the hell *do* you know? What's this crap about some over-the-hill fed who's after me in his spare time 'cause his kid went when we wasted Marcellino?"

"I heard it from a very reliable source."

"*Bullshit.* You saying this one old fart can cause me trouble?" The Emperor sneered. *"Me?"*

"I'm not saying. I'm *asking.* Do you really want to find out? The hard way? Or do you want to stop him now?"

Patrovita paused to consider the question.

"We might as well get rid of him," he replied. "You wanna do it?"

"Don't be preposterous."

Then Keller spoke.

"Let Brenner hit him."

"And then Brenner goes," Patrovita said. "Good idea, Max. Do it yourself."

Keller smiled.

"Be a pleasure, Mr. Patrovita," he exulted.

The man in the shadows frowned. He didn't enjoy this kind of talk. He didn't even want to hear it. He sold information, and he'd rather not think about the distasteful consequences.

"I have to go," he announced.

They heard his footsteps recede . . . silence.

"The fed's name is Harry Shannon," Patrovita said. "Works out of the Bureau office downtown. I want you to *retire* him—and Brenner—in the next coupla days."

"You got it," Keller promised eagerly.

As they left the funeral parlor by the rear exit to the alley, Patrovita's thoughts turned to Rocca. They'd been together for a long time. Now Rocca was starting to make mistakes. Instead of solving the goddamn problems he was becoming part of them.

First he let this bastard Brenner sucker him.

Then he argued with Luigi Patrovita about recovering the money and dope.

The Emperor didn't like mistakes or arguments. He'd never had either from Carl Rocca before. Maybe Carl was getting too old for the job.

Hell, they might have to retire him too.

39

Lots of people are still asleep at eight-thirty on a Sunday morning.

Joey Brenner wasn't.

He was finishing shaving when he heard the pounding on his apartment door.

Straight razor still in his hand, he walked from the bathroom to meet his visitor. He stopped to pick up the Beretta before he proceeded to the door.

He didn't stand in front of it. That's how you could catch a shotgun blast through the thin wooden panel. He paused just beside the door before he spoke.

"Who is it?"

"Max. Open up."

The ex-F.B.I. agent unhooked the chain, released the lock. Keller marched in, saw the razor and the pistol, and grinned broadly.

"Who're you expecting, Joey? King Kong?"

His tone was cheerful, but the poison was still in his eyes.

"What's up?" Brenner asked.

"You can put down the razor—but keep the gun. We've got another job to do. Won't take long. You can get to church later." The man who liked killing chuckled.

Joey Brenner immediately realized that something was wrong.

The cheery good humor was a fake.

Why the sham? Why this morning?

"Who're we hitting?" he asked as he reached for his shirt.

"Nobody you know. Hurry up. Freddy's waiting in the car."

Another killing?

Mark Kaminski hadn't bargained for this.

He was no murderer.

There must be some way for him to avoid slaying the anonymous victim. Even if the target was another vicious gangster like Lamansky, Kaminski didn't want to do it. He'd think of something on the way . . . or when they got there. He had to.

Max Keller was humming as they left the apartment. He was pleased that The Emperor liked his idea, and delighted that all his humiliation would soon be avenged. He glanced furtively at Brenner for just a moment. Keller decided that he'd blow his enemy's face off. That would teach the blond bitch a lesson if she came to look at the boy.

They saw her as soon as they stepped out of the building. Monique Tyler wasn't wearing her usual glamour garb. Instead she had on jeans and a bulky jacket and a look of weary sadness.

"Be right with you, Max," Brenner assured as he hurried to meet her.

"Make it fast. We can't be late for this picnic," the hit man warned.

When Brenner reached her, she spoke first.

"I'm sorry about the other night. I wanted . . . you see . . . Christ, where would I learn to deal with a *friend*? I haven't had one in years, Joey."

"It's okay."

"I came over . . . Look, I thought we could talk."

"I have something to do. We'll talk later."

He could see that she wasn't sure she could believe him.

"Scout's honor. Take my car and go home," he said as he handed her the keys. "I'll phone as soon as I'm back."

She noticed Keller watching them from ten yards away. The ugly smile on his face suddenly infuriated her, and she grabbed Joey Brenner. She kissed him full on the mouth—long and hard.

Keller seemed amused, not angry.

His face still had that mean grin as he shook his head twice.

Why was he so smug?

She was still wondering when Keller and Brenner got into the dark blue sedan and drove away. Keller drove through the semideserted streets of the sprawling city carefully, chatting with Freddy Wheeler in the backseat. Wheeler, whose two gold teeth the undercover cop remembered from their meeting in the subterranean casino, was a wonderful listener. He appreciated every one of Max Keller's obscene jokes, racist remarks, and raucous boasts of alleged sexual prowess.

He had to.

Keller—the man in charge—didn't let him get in a word sideways.

Not up or down, either.

He was in unusually genial and expansive spirits throughout the fifty-minute drive to the Mount Xavier Cemetery. Keller didn't notice the car following them. He guided the sedan through the open gates and turned up the road that branched off to the left. Then he cruised slowly, obviously looking for someone or something.

"Funny place for a picnic," Joey Brenner tested.

Keller didn't reply. His eyes roved back and forth, searching urgently. He was looking ahead. Off to the right a score of mourners clustered in a graveside farewell. Farther up the driveway on the left, a pair of stolid men in work clothes were digging a new grave for a midday funeral.

Brenner realized the reason for Max Keller's concentration. He was so intense because the hit would take place in this cemetery . . . within the next few minutes. The victim was probably within two or three hundred yards of them.

I'll shoot to miss with the first round, he thought.

Maybe the target would escape.

Or Keller would do the job and mock Joey Brenner for poor marksmanship.

The dark blue sedan rolled ahead at five miles an hour.

"There he is," Keller announced.

The man they'd come to murder was kneeling in front of a headstone forty yards away. His back was to the car. It was impossible to identify him.

"Out, Freddy," Keller ordered.

Wheeler swiftly checked the loads in his sawed-off shotgun, concealed it under his raincoat, and left the sedan. He began to circle the kneeling man as the car inched forward.

"Who is he, Max?" Brenner asked.

"Just a fuckin' cop," the homicidal hoodlum replied as he stopped the vehicle.

The nightmare was happening.

Here and now.

The worst that Mark Kaminski had feared was upon him.

"You go straight at him, Joey. I'll take the right."

Wheeler was getting into firing position on the left.

They'd attack from three sides—simultaneously—with a deadly crossfire. The nameless cop wouldn't have a chance.

Unless Mark Kaminski risked everything to save him.

He had about ten seconds to decide.

He made his choice in three.

He drew the Beretta, held it flat against his coat, and kept walking. When he was twenty-five feet from the target, the kneeling man stood up and turned.

Brenner stared.

It was Shannon.

"Harry," he gasped.

Now Max Keller pulled out his .357 Magnum and shouted.

"Kill him!"

Shannon took in the situation in an instant. He dropped to one knee—just in time to miss a blast from Wheeler's shotgun. Shannon had his own weapon in his hand, and the veteran federal agent knew exactly what to do.

His bullet tore the sleeve of Keller's coat a moment before the .357 smashed a gaping hole in the FBI man's left shoulder. Then Brenner and Wheeler fired. The shotgun pellets ripped into Harry Shannon's side, knocking him down. He was badly wounded.

Wheeler wasn't.

He was dead. One of the undercover cop's bullets opened his throat like a spigot, squirting blood a foot. The other tore into his brain.

As the corpse fell, the eight-round shotgun fell to the graveled path. The impact knocked it to "automatic." It began firing, blowing away pieces of headstones and spraying random death into the sunny morning.

Terrified people nearby were screaming . . . scattering. One sensible 170-pound widow jumped into the open grave beside her, knocking a startled priest into the hole too. Rigid with fear and unable to flee, other mourners began to pray.

Max Keller didn't see any of this.

He was busy getting ready to kill Joey Brenner. He had his enemy in his sights. His finger tightened on the trigger. Harry Shannon's finger was quicker. Slumped against his son's headstone, the half-dead FBI man shot him in the stomach.

Keller staggered.

But he didn't drop his weapon. He knew that he was finished, but he'd take Joey Brenner down the long slide to nowhere with him. With his belly a ball of searing pain, he lifted the Magnum.

That was when Mark Kaminski killed him.

Two shots to the heart.

The slugs hurled him back against a headstone, and he crumpled over the slab of marble. The body hung draped over it for five . . . six . . . seven seconds before it rolled off onto a neatly tended grave.

The corpse lay there, faceup. Max Keller had been an ugly man when he was alive. Dying didn't improve his looks at all.

Kaminski ran to his fallen friend.

"I didn't know it was you, Harry."

"It's okay. Jeezus Christ, it hurts."

His face was white . . . his clothes soaked with blood.

More was seeping from the wounds every second.

"I'll call an ambulance, Harry."

"Not from here. Get out—now. If I don't make it and the cops take you, you'll never talk your way out of this."

"I'm not leaving you, Harry."

The man on the ground winced in pain.

"You've got to," he said. "You've got to finish this. There's stuff you may need in a suitcase in the safe house. Take it."

"You're going to make it, Harry," Kaminski insisted.

"You're a lousy liar," Shannon whispered. "Get out of here and give 'em hell. *Promise*?"

A siren sounded in the distance.

"Promise," Mark Kaminski vowed.

Then he ran for the car. When he reached it, he saw that the keys weren't in the ignition. Keller had them. The siren was getting louder. He was running out of time.

As he turned to spring back to Keller's corpse, a car horn blasted thirty yards away. He looked around to see his Cadillac barreling down the narrow road toward him. Monique Tyler was at the wheel.

She slammed the brakes, screeched to a halt beside him.

"What the hell are you doing here?" he demanded loudly as he jumped in beside her.

"Saving your ass, friend."

There were more sirens.

She gunned the engine, and the Cadillac roared away. They didn't speak until the cemetery was two miles behind them.

"Thanks," he said simply.

"That's what friends are for," she replied. "You're lucky this friend thought Max Keller looked like he was up to something dirty, Joey. That's why I followed you out there."

"*Very* lucky," he agreed. "By the way, nobody has to worry about Max anymore."

"*Ever?*"

"Until hell freezes over. He's there now."

"I don't supposes you wanna tell me what happened," she said, thinking aloud.

"You really don't want to know. Mind if I drive?"

She stopped the car, and he took her place behind the wheel. When they reached the lofty apartment tower where she lived, he reached across to open the passenger door beside her.

"No questions," he said as he took out his wallet and gave her a fistful of Harry Shannon's money. "There's no time. Pack whatever you can't live without—fast. Get out to the Rock Falls airport and charter a plane."

"To where?"

"It's *when* that counts. If you want to live, you'd better be airborne within ninety minutes."

"Where are you going?" she asked.

"Out to the gravel pit. Where is it?"

"Don't do it, Joey!" she pleaded.

"Where is it?"

"Pearson Road—just this side of Cicero. For God's sake, Joey, what are you going to do there?"

"What another friend asked me to: Give 'em hell!"

She kissed him, and then she got out of the car.

"Good-bye, friend," he said.

He put the Cadillac in gear. She watched it until it was out of sight.

40

*H*e drove directly to the grubby building that housed Shannon's "safe" apartment. He hurried upstairs, popped open the lock with a credit card, and went in to find the suitcase.

He looked around but couldn't see it anywhere. Then he noticed the closet. He tried the door. It was locked. It was a key job. The credit card stunt only worked on snap locks.

Kaminski studied the wooden door for a few seconds.

Then he smashed his fist right through the center panel.

He reached inside, opened the door, and took out the cheap nylon case. He decided to open it back at his apartment. He had a pretty good idea as to what was in it. He picked it up, felt the weight, and nodded.

"Thanks, Harry," he said.

When he got down to his car, he found a fat, swarthy man trying to open it with a screwdriver.

"Don't do that," Kaminski said irritably.

The auto thief turned with a curse, raising the screwdriver

like a dagger. Shaking his head in disgust, the undercover cop caught the wrist of the hand holding the weapon, swung the thief around in a wide circle, and threw him headfirst into a brick wall.

As the unconscious man fell, Kaminski got into the Cadillac and flicked on the radio. He listened to an all-news station as he drove to his own apartment. In a breathless baritone an announcer was rattling off a report on the "shocking" shoot-out at the cemetery. Two men were dead. A "gravely wounded federal agent was in Cook County Hospital—fighting for his life."

The gravel pit would have to wait.

When he neared the hospital, he saw three police cars in the parking lot. He circled around to the rear of the building, parked the Cadillac in a spot marked DOCTORS ONLY, and walked quickly to a rear door. The credit card worked again.

The corridors of the busy public hospital were alive with orderlies, nurses, interns, technicians, and a colorful assortment of people visiting sick friends and relatives. Kaminski had no idea of the building's layout or where Shannon might be.

And he had very little time.

If his hunch was right, the gravel pit that Monique Tyler's late husband wouldn't dare talk about housed a key Patrovita operation—something a lot more important than a gambling casino. He had to get there before The Emperor even considered reinforcing it. With dangerous and deadly Joey Brenner on the rampage, that would be a logical precaution.

Kaminski saw a nurse's station ten yards away. The woman in white was arguing with an orderly. When she turned away, Kaminski walked boldly to the desk and picked up the phone.

"This is Dr. Stoltz," he said authoritatively to the switchboard operator. "Is Mr. Shannon out of the OR yet?... I see.... Room 316. Thank you."

The nurse turned. He looked at her with the lordly glance that physicians regularly bestow on lesser beings in hospitals, and she shrugged.

Another arrogant bastard, she thought, and went back to chewing out the orderly.

Kaminski strode importantly down the hall, turned the corner, and saw the door marked LINEN & SUPPLY. He slipped inside quickly. When he emerged three minutes later, he was dressed in an orderly's uniform—just a bit tight. It would have to do.

He walked up the service stairway to the third floor. As he stepped out, a pair of uniformed police walked past, and he followed them. He checked the room numbers as he did. 304 ... 306 ... 308.

Room 316 was around the next corner.

Another orderly came by, holding a vase filled with flowers. Kaminski saw him stop outside a door marked MEN, hesitate, and put down the vase on a wheeled cart. When the orderly went inside to relieve his kidneys, Kaminski scooped up the vase and hurried on to room 316.

A cop stood guard outside.

"Would you please take these in to Mr. Shannon?" Kaminski asked.

"Sure."

The policeman opened the door, and Kaminski slipped in right behind him. As the door closed, Kaminski jerked the cop's gun from its holster. Both the policeman and the nurse seated beside the bed looked stunned.

Harry Shannon looked a lot worse. He lay pale and semiconscious, with intravenous tubes and other life-support systems plugged into his ravaged body. An electronic monitor beside him flashed graphic evidence that his heart was still working.

Kaminski pointed the gun.

"Not a word. Both of you—over there against the wall."

They obeyed. Kaminski leaned down close to Shannon's ear.

"Harry? Harry, do you hear me?"

Shannon struggled to open his eyes. They looked disoriented . . . fuzzed by the sedatives. He fought to focus.

"Mark? Did you get him?" he asked weakly.

"That's what I came to tell you. I'm on my way."

"Me too," Shannon mumbled. "I think I'm dying."

"You can't. You've got to hang in until I nail him. Just a couple of hours, Harry."

"Too late. They know about you. You'll never get near him. It's over."

"*The hell it is.* I'm gonna bring you his goddamn head on a plate," Kaminski vowed. "It's for Blair, Harry."

He mentioned the murdered son quite deliberately.

Maybe hate could keep the critically wounded FBI agent alive.

"Don't let go," Kaminski urged. "Think about Blair. Hang in."

"I'll try, but—"

Suddenly Shannon's eyes widened and seemed to roll up into their sockets. His body shook and his hands clawed at the sheets.

A chilling sound filled the room.

The wavy lines on the heart monitor were straight as the machine emitted a steady beep.

"Cardiac arrest!" the nurse shouted.

"Do something, dammit!" Kaminski yelled.

Seeing him distracted, the policeman rushed to disarm him. Kaminski dropped him with a punch, opened the door, and saw the other two cops. They spotted the gun he held immediately. They pulled their own weapons.

He spun back into the room. He wasn't going to shoot any police . . . and he wasn't going to be captured.

Not yet.

Not until he destroyed Luigi Patrovita.

There was one way out and he took it.

He dived through the window.

Below, an orderly wheeling a hamper filled with laundry was astounded when Kaminski tumbled into it with a crash and knocked it over. Shaken but undamaged, Kaminski climbed out, looked around, and ran for his car.

He'd been lucky to fall onto laundry that cushioned his fall.

Would his luck hold out in the battle ahead?

41

*M*ark Kaminski drove back to his apartment where he stripped swiftly. He didn't need to dress like Joey Brenner anymore. Brenner was as dead as those bastards he'd left at the cemetery.

It was open warfare now.

Time to dress for battle.

He donned comfortable jeans, a T-shirt, and hiking boots. Then he opened Shannon's suitcase. He wasn't disappointed. It was filled with ammunition and an assortment of first-class weapons.

An MP-5K submachine gun, the devastating 9-millimeter blaster used by both the U.S. Rangers and Britain's elite SAS commandos for overwhelming firepower.

Also, 750 rounds of Parabellum death per minute.

And half a dozen thirty-round magazines.

A pump-action Winchester 1200 shotgun—with a box of three-inch Magnum loads and an ammunition belt.

A pair of heavy Browning Hi-Power pistols—with ten clips.

He loaded the guns and filled the ammo belt with extra

shotgun shells. Then he slung the belt over one shoulder. After stuffing two clips of pistol ammunition in each pocket, he slipped sweatbands onto his wrists.

Now he was ready to go to war.

He drove toward Cicero, got the location of Pearson Road from a gas station attendant, and found it without difficulty. Half a mile off the highway he saw the sign beside a locked gate: ABC GRAVEL.

He shot off the lock with the submachine gun. Then he swung to blow out the entire windshield of the Cadillac. Now he had the total visibility that he needed.

Some three hundred yards away, a Patrovita sentry atop one of the long conveyors heard the sounds and grabbed his walkie-talkie.

"This is Pete. I think I heard shooting."

Another armed guard was lying on his stomach at the crest of a small mountain of crushed gravel a hundred and twenty yards beyond. He peered up the road intently before he replied.

"I don't see nothin,' Pete."

The Cadillac suddenly swept into view.

It raced toward the conveyor at forty miles an hour.

"There's a car coming like a rocket. Could be Lamansky's crew!" the sentry on the conveyor radioed.

Half a mile a way, seven armed men were working in a small corrugated-metal shed. They were cutting and bagging the heroin taken from the police station. The sacks of currency rested on the floor beside them.

There was an eighth hoodlum monitoring the radio. He heard the warning and jumped to his feet.

"Outside! Outside—on the double! It's Lamansky's mob!"

They seized their weapons, rushed out, and scattered to take up firing positions in a wide arc.

The man on the conveyor rose and took careful aim at the big car. Brenner swung the submachine gun. A short burst chopped the sentry from his perch. His remains bounced on the loose gravel below.

All of Patrovita's "soldiers" were firing as fast as they could, trying to stop the zigzagging Cadillac that just kept coming. Kaminski hit the brakes, spun the heavy car expertly, and poured back deadly fire.

First through one window. Then the other.

As the Caddy passed the shed one of the gunmen stepped forward and blew the rear window out. Kaminski spun the car like a stunt driver again, turned in his seat, and put five rounds into the hoodlum beside the shed.

Bullets were crashing into the car from all sides. One seared his left cheek. Another sliced a shallow groove an inch long on his right arm. As the Cadillac swept around one of the mini-peaks of gravel, a potbellied thug stepped forward to fire directly into Kaminski's face.

His aim wasn't quite good enough.

Mark Kaminski's was better.

The heavy car ran right over him, crushing ribs . . . arms . . . legs . . . and vital organs instantly. Off to the left, two other hoodlums were scaling a mound to get a better field of fire. The rapid-fire MP-5K knocked them down with short, surgically precise bursts.

One struggled to his feet groggily, looking for the Smith and Wesson .38 he'd dropped. Kaminski pulled up alongside as the hoodlum found the gun. The undercover cop lifted one of the twin Browning Hi-Powers that Shannon had provided and swung it swiftly.

The range was point-blank.

The death was quick.

Kaminski bulled ahead another hundred yards before he put the car into a tight turn. Then he saw the huge vehicle moving toward him. The Terex Pit Truck was a monster no bullets could stop. He twisted the wheel violently to spin the car off in the opposite direction.

Another mechanical giant was grinding toward him. It was a massive Caterpillar loader. He'd run out of room to maneuver. There was no place to dodge. Bullets were raking the Cadillac from three directions. The two enormous vehicles were closing in steadily.

Thirty yards.

Twenty yards.

Ten.

He jerked open the door beside him, grabbed the shotgun, and rolled out seconds before the Cadillac was crushed between the monsters. Those machines' drivers were shouting in triumph, unaware that he wasn't inside being pulped.

They found out when he raised the shotgun and blew away one-third of the Caterpillar jockey's head. The Terex pulled back with a menacing grinding noise. Then its driver rammed it forward again to obliterate the invader.

Kaminski began the run. The huge machine pursued him. Its driver poured on more speed. Kaminski reached the metal shed and sliced gashes in the skin with the submachine gun until the clip was exhausted.

Now the enormous truck was moving in for the kill. He ran as fast as he could, his heart pounding as he heard the Terex closing the gap.

Nearer . . . nearer.

Then he seemed to stumble, and the truck driver blew a loud blast on his deafening horn in celebration. Kaminski fell. The gigantic Terex passed right over him.

But it didn't kill him.

A moment before it reached him he rolled *between* the huge wheels. As soon as it chugged on, he leapt to his feet to charge the shed again. The three men inside fired back frantically as he advanced.

Holding the shotgun at his hip, he smashed one Magnum load into the chest of a hoodlum standing in the doorway. Kaminski ripped three more shells from the ammo belt, reloaded the stainless-steel-barreled Winchester 1200, and came on blasting. Working the pump action with stunning speed, he vaulted onto the loading dock and spun.

The heavy shotgun crashed again and again.

He reloaded, fired and fired.

The two men inside were riddled with shot at close range. They tottered, screaming as they fell onto the heroin and sacks of money. They moaned for a few seconds, twisted in pain, and perished.

Kaminski eyed the carnage for several moments. Heroin scattered everywhere...bloodstained currency in clumps...a pair of shotgun-ravaged corpses on the floor. There was an awful sickness in this place, he thought.

Then he heard the noise once more.

The immense Terex was coming back to kill him.

He looked out, saw it heading straight for the shed.

It weighed many tons. Nothing could stop it.

Kaminski drew the twin Hi-Powers, dropped into a shooter's crouch, and took careful aim. He squeezed both triggers.

The 9-millimeter slugs caught the driver in the eyes, tearing out the back of his skull as they exited. There was a corpse on the floor of the giant truck's cab, but it kept coming.

Then the mighty motor sputtered...gurgled...stopped.

Three feet from the shed's doorway where Kaminski stood, the Terex died—of hunger. When the driver's foot slid from the gas pedal, the fuel supply dwindled and halted.

But the battle wasn't finished.

Three more of Patrovita's guards who's been on duty on the other side of the gravel pit were moving toward him in an armored truck. He had no ammunition that could pierce the steel plate. Bullets flew all around him.

His eyes swept the area.

Maybe.

He lifted the pistols again and fired at the cable that led to an immense tipple filled with gravel.

He missed.

The armored truck was moving in for the kill.

He raised the Brownings again, aimed, and pulled the triggers.

The cable snapped.

With a thunderous roar, thirty-eight tons of gravel crashed down onto the armored truck—squashing it like a lightweight aluminum beer can.

More gravel poured down. The mound grew higher and higher.

It finally shuddered and snarled to a halt.

There was nothing alive under that enormous weight, Mark Kaminski thought. There couldn't be. The gravel heap stood twenty or twenty-one feet high. It might take two days to remove the mangled remains from under that tomb, he speculated.

It took three and a half.

42

People stared.

Chicago is known as the City with Big Shoulders.

Even in Chicago this machine attracted attention.

The huge Terex rolled down the street like a tidal wave. Everyone and everything got out of its way. It swung around the corner with its earsplitting air horn blasting warning.

The message was clear.

Nothing was going to stop it, and it would stop for no one.

When Kaminski saw the hotel, he applied the powerful brakes, and the awesome juggernaut crunched to a halt in front of the entrance. The uniformed doorman peered at the monster uneasily. He'd never seen a behemoth like this in downtown Chicago before.

Kaminski sounded the air horn again.

The frightened doorman jumped. Then he saw the man at the wheel climb down. The driver was a good-looking, angry-faced man loaded with an astonishing arsenal. Shotgun . . . submachine gun . . . twin pistols in his belt. He had the stride and muscular body of a top athlete—and a hundred-dollar bill in his right hand.

"Don't bother to park it," he announced as he gave the bug-eyed doorman the large bill. "I'll only be a minute."

Mark Kaminski walked through the lobby to the elevators, ignoring the bewildered glances of the shaken guests around him. When he pressed the down button, nothing happened. There wasn't even a light.

"The casino's closed," a bellboy confided.

"Not anymore," Kaminski corrected.

He pointed the shotgun at the button and blew it out of the wall. As if intimidated, the elevator door opened. That was five seconds before the bellboy panicked and ran out into the street screaming.

There were fifteen men in the gambling club below. A dozen were The Emperor's heavily armed bodyguards. Two more were Luigi Patrovita, himself, and Carl Rocca. The other was the man who had betrayed Marcellino and the federal agents to the hired killers.

They all heard the noise of the shotgun.

They turned and saw the light indicating that the elevator was descending.

"It has to be Brenner," Rocca said.

"Blast him while he's still in the elevator," Patrovita ordered.

The bodyguards fanned out obediently, pointed their guns at the elevator door, and waited. When the floor-indicator sign signaled that the elevator cab had arrived, they all opened fire. They riddled the door and scourged the elevator cab behind it with nearly a hundred rounds.

Nothing could survive that fusillade.

That was what they found when the door opened.

Nothing.

And no one. The cab was empty.

Where had the son of a bitch vanished to?

Was he man or ghost?

Fingers on their triggers, the men in the casino nervously scanned in one direction . . . then another. Suddenly they heard the sound of something heavy sliding over a metal surface. It seemed to be coming from everywhere.

It stopped abruptly.

A three-foot-square metal grille covering the overhead air-recirculating shaft popped open, and the man they knew as Joey Brenner dropped from the duct like a cat—feetfirst. He had a Browning Hi-Power in one hand, a submachine gun in the other.

Both boomed immediately. Sweeping across the room like a scythe, the automatic weapon cut down three . . . four . . . five of the bodyguards in seconds. The others were firing wildly, trying to find him in the haze of acrid smoke. Two stepped forward looking for him. He killed them with single shots from the pistol.

Bullets ravaged furniture, smashed mirrors and television screens, and desecrated the elegant walls with scores of holes. Fragments of shattered glasses and liquor bottles behind the bar sprayed out like shrapnel.

"There he is!" Patrovita yelled.

The Emperor was firing a big .45 revolver. Four of the bodyguards charged in the direction in which he'd pointed. Mark Kaminski stepped out from behind a pillar off to the right, swung the rapid-fire MP-5K, and sent three of them to meet Max Keller in hell.

The surviving bodyguard dropped to the floor to offer a minimum target. He lay there tautly for several seconds, making no sound. Kaminski didn't move, either. When the hoodlum finally raised his head above a table to make a wary inspection, the "dead" sheriff emptied both pistols into his chest, driving his lifeless body back into a chair.

The Emperor was no fool.

With all his bodyguards killed, he'd be crazy to stay around to face the brutally efficient "Brenner."

"Cover me, Carl," he shouted, and ran for the elevator.

Rocca fired as fast as he could, falling back toward the shaft that meant survival. Kaminski had discarded the empty pistols. He had the pump-action shotgun in his hands as he relentlessly pursued the last two of his enemies.

Rocca caught a blast in the stomach and staggered back howling into the elevator five seconds before it closed. Patrovita shouted a curse from within. That was when the ex-FBI man pumped the Winchester twice more. When the elevator door opened at the lobby floor, there were two dead men inside. One was Carl Rocca. They had to look at the other corpse's wallet to identify him. The two rounds from the Winchester had obliterated five-sixths of Luigi Patrovita's features.

It was quiet in the casino now.

Kaminski reloaded the shotgun automatically, taking no chances.

Maybe they weren't all dead.

There could be others alive—hiding.

Winchester at the ready, he warily scanned the ruined room. It was littered with debris—human and other. He saw nothing move. Was it finally finished?

He heard the sound. A whimper—barely human.

It came from a man down on his hands and knees, picking up abandoned gun after abandoned gun. As he found each was out of bullets, he dropped it like a petulant child and groped for another.

He wasn't a child.

He was a forty-two-year-old man whom Mark Kaminski knew.

Yes, he had to be the traitor who'd sold Blair Shannon and the others.

The former FBI agent walked toward him slowly. He ought to kill him right now. Whether Harry Shannon was still alive or not, Mark Kaminski owed him that. Kaminski stepped closer, and his shadow fell on the sniveling creature on the floor.

The man in the rumpled business suit looked up, blinked.

No, it wasn't possible.

"Kaminski?" he asked uncertainly.

"That's right, Mr. Baxter."

The spy was the same bastard who had so righteously ruined Mark Kaminski's career in New York three years ago—holier-than-anyone Marvin Baxter.

"You believe in poetic justice, Mr. Baxter? No, you don't believe in any kind of justice, you son of a bitch!"

"You don't understand," the celebrated prosecutor protested shrilly. "I was collecting evidence against these criminals. Building an airtight case. I pretended to go along to find out . . . you know . . . I fooled them . . . For God's sake, don't look at me like that!"

"I don't want to look at you at all. No one else will, either, after today. Why don't you save the government some money?" Kaminski demanded.

He picked up a .38 automatic, checked the clip, and handed it to Baxter.

"It's this or fifty years in jail with guys who don't like district attorneys—some guys you put inside."

The corrupt lawyer babbled on hysterically.

"So you're back with the Bureau . . . it was a misunderstanding . . . doing my job . . . nothing personal."

"You gave me a choice. Resign or be prosecuted," Mark

Kaminski harshly reminded him. "Now it's your turn to choose. A quick good-bye or being gang-raped every night until you don't care anymore."

Baxter wasn't uttering words.

Nonsense syllables were all that came from his twisted mouth.

Suddenly he stopped, stared at the pistol in silence for several seconds.

"No jail," he croaked.

"Say hello to Max Keller," the man with the shotgun said, and started for the elevator.

The prosecutor turned the muzzle of the pistol toward his own chest . . . hesitated.

Kaminski kept walking, expecting the sound of the suicide shot any moment. He heard the gun go off—twice. Bullets gouged chunks from the wall beside Kaminski's ear. Marvin Baxter had made his choice.

Kaminski made his—very easily. He turned, and the shotgun boomed twice. Then Kaminski reloaded in pure reflex and the pump-action Winchester thundered again . . . and again . . . and again.

The impact of five shotgun rounds sent Baxter cartwheeling back as if he were an acrobat. The fifth round didn't hit Baxter. It merely savaged his remains.

Mark Kaminski stared at the body.

"Thanks," he said.

Then he reloaded the 12-gauge weapon as he walked toward the elevator. There was one more thing that he had to take care of today. He hoped that no one would get in his way. He didn't want to shoot anyone else this afternoon.

43

Wall-to-wall cops.

The ruined casino was crowded with all kinds of police.

Two of them were Detective Sergeant Ira Baker and his young partner. Carson didn't look as eager as usual. His expression was more one of awe. Scanning the wreckage, the body bags, and the general devastation, he shook his head.

"Holy shit!" he said for the tenth time.

"At least," the older detective replied.

"One man did all this? What kind of man could do all this by himself?"

"A liar," Baker replied. "He told us he was *clean*, remember?"

A red-haired cop emerged from the elevator and hurried toward them.

"Just got a flash on the radio, Sarge. They've spotted an '85 Rolls registered to Patrovita cruising south on Route 84. Should they bag it?"

"Maintain surveillance and keep me informed," Baker answered. "Route 84?"

"What is it?" Carson asked.

"Either a great hunch or a small mistake. Let's find out."

Out at the Rock Falls Airport Monique Tyler watched the twin-turboprop charter plane move toward her. As it drew near she heard a powerful engine hum behind her and turned to see a Rolls-Royce. It was coming right at her.

She was startled when "Joey Brenner" emerged from the $80,000 vehicle with a large sack.

"You coming with me?" she asked hopefully.

"Can't. Here's a going-away present."

He handed her the bag that he'd taken from the gravel pit shed.

"There's half a million of Patrovita's dollars in this," he told her. "You can use it for a fresh start. A new name . . . a new life . . . far away from this part of the country."

"I want to stay with you, Joey."

"You don't know me, Monique. You don't even know my right name. I'm not Joey Brenner and I'm not from Chicago."

"Who the hell are you?"

"I'm a cop."

She looked dumbfounded.

"Scout's honor?" she asked incredulously.

"Scout's honor."

She glared for a long moment before she grinned.

"So I've got a cop friend. So long, friend."

There was a noise overhead now.

Kaminski glanced up, recognized the police markings on the approaching helicopter.

"So long," he replied.

He carried her suitcase and the sack of cash to the

turboprop and watched it lift off the runway two minutes later. The rotor craft touched down. Detective Ira Baker emerged.

"I figured it was you in the Rolls," he announced.

"I like to go in style."

Baker shook his head.

"What kind of style was that number you did at the goddamn casino? Early Attila the Hun? I've seen train wrecks that were prettier," he announced. "What a mess you left us!"

"Nobody said there were points for neatness," Kaminski answered.

"And it's gonna take days to clean up the other mess at the gravel pit. I don't even wanna think about the legal thing. Man, you trashed laws that aren't even on the books yet. Come on. Someone wants to see you, Mark."

"Who told you my name?"

"Your old buddy in Cook County."

"Harry made it!" Kaminski exulted.

"He likes you too," Baker said wryly. "That's why he told us. Didn't want some cop blowing you away before you finished World War Three."

Kaminski was grinning as they walked to the helicopter.

He didn't give a damn who wanted to see him or what price he'd have to pay for what he'd done.

Patrovita was dead and his crime syndicate demolished.

And Harry Shannon was *alive*.

Mark Kaminski had kept his promise.

44

*M*ark Kaminski didn't go to jail.
He went to Washington instead.

The Director of the Bureau was very proud of him—sort of. That's what an assistant director told Mark Kaminski after the mayor of Chicago said that Kaminski should get a medal. Some twenty-six senators, a dozen governors, and Johnny Carson said the same thing.

The director was too busy to see Kaminski himself. A highly intelligent man, he was playing it safe until he found out how the president felt about this bizarre situation.

Unprecedented.

Never in the history of the Bureau.

So the assistant director greeted Mr. and Mrs. Kaminski and posed for a picture with them—and told Mark Kaminski that he was being reinstated. After all, the entire case against Mark Kaminski was probably tainted because who could really accept anything that the late Mr. Baxter had done or said?

And Mark Kaminski was being assigned to the Kansas City FBI office—as of next week.

"New York," Amy Kaminski said.

She spoke in a loud, clear, polite, but definitely no-nonsense voice.

"New York—or he'll write a book about *all* this," she threatened. Her handsome husband nodded.

"New York? No problem," the assistant director assured her.

45

Nine weeks later Harry Shannon visited the Kaminskis in their new apartment on Manhattan's Upper West Side—a few blocks north of the lively Lincoln Center for the Performing Arts. The FBI man couldn't help but notice how she glowed with enthusiasm after the all-Mozart concert that afternoon.

She was still talking about the splendid music when the three of them finished dinner in the Kaminski apartment. When it was time for Shannon to go, Mark Kaminski walked Shannon to the door.

"Blair can rest now," the older man said. "Thanks, Mark."

"I owe you thanks too. Wouldn't be back in the Bureau if you hadn't come up with that idea."

"It was crazy, wasn't it?" Shannon reflected.

"A little," Kaminski answered as he handed him an envelope.

"What's this, Mark?"

"Your change: $31,280 I never spent."

Shannon shook his head, put the fat envelope in the

inside pocket of his Donegal tweed jacket, and shook his gray head again.

"I really like you," he said, "but I still don't like the way you do things. I don't want to hurt your feelings, but why can't you operate like ordinary people?"

"If I find out, I'll drop you a card," Kaminski replied cheerfully.

After Shannon left, Mark Kaminski told his wife what the older man had said.

"You want me to act like ordinary people?" he asked.

She smiled mischievously as she pointed to the bedroom doorway.

"Be extraordinary, Mark," she urged.

He was.

GREAT MEN'S ADVENTURE

__DIRTY HARRY
by Dane Hartman

Never before published or seen on screen.

He's "Dirty Harry" Callahan—tough, unorthodox, no-nonsense plain-clothesman extraordinaire of the San Francisco Police Department . . . Inspector #71 assigned to the bruising, thankless homicide detail . . . A consummate crimebuster nothing can stop—not even the law!

__DEATH ON THE DOCKS   (C90-792, $1.95)

__MASSACRE AT RUSSIAN RIVER (C30-052, $1.95)

__NINJA MASTER
by Wade Barker

Committed to avenging injustice, Brett Wallace uses the ancient Japanese art of killing as he stalks the evildoers of the world in his mission.

__SKIN SWINDLE   (C30-227, $1.95)

__ONLY THE GOOD DIE   (C30-239, $2.25)

WARNER BOOKS
P.O. Box 690
New York, N.Y. 10019

Please send me the books I have checked. I enclose a check or money order (not cash), plus 50¢ per order and 50¢ per copy to cover postage and handling.* (Allow 4 weeks for delivery.)

_____ Please send me your free mail order catalog. (If ordering only the catalog, include a large self-addressed, stamped envelope.)

Name _____

Address _____

City _____

State _____ Zip _____

*N.Y. State and California residents add applicable sales tax.   14

DETECTIVE PETER BRAGG MYSTERY SERIES WILL EXPLODE OFF YOUR SHELVES!

Tough, gritty, authentic, packed with action and loaded with danger, Jack Lynch's BRAGG novels are American hard-boiled detective fiction in the grand tradition of Hammett and Chandler.

___**SAUSALITO**   (B32-083, $2.95, U.S.A.)
by Jack Lynch   (B32-084, $3.75, Canada)

Peter Bragg, working on a blackmail case in the quiet community of Sausalito, senses something else simmering beneath the ocean-kissed beachfront. Residents are being "persuaded" to give up their homes to the developers of a glittering new hotel complex. Bragg smells a conspiracy so immense that his own life isn't worth a paper dollar if he doesn't bring the criminals to justice. And if anybody can, Bragg will.

___**SAN QUENTIN**   (B32-085, $2.95, U.S.A.)
by Jack Lynch   (B32-086, $3.75, Canada)

It's mayhem in maximum security at San Quentin State Prison. Right now, it's a battlefield with guards on one side of a barricade and a group of hostage-holding cons on the other. Their incredible demand? Let their leader's kid brother off a murder rap—or else . . . The case is a natural for Bragg. It's a dangerous, down-and-dirty job—and only Bragg can stop the bloodbath.

WARNER BOOKS
P.O. Box 690
New York, N.Y. 10019

Please send me the books I have checked. I enclose a check or money order (not cash), plus 50¢ per order and 50¢ per copy to cover postage and handling.* (Allow 4 weeks for delivery.)

_____ Please send me your free mail order catalog. (If ordering only the catalog, include a large self-addressed, stamped envelope.)

Name _____

Address _____

City _____

State _____ Zip _____

*N.Y. State and California residents add applicable sales tax.   108

By the year 2000, 2 out of 3 Americans could be illiterate.

It's true.

Today, 75 million adults... about one American in three, can't read adequately. And by the year 2000, U.S. News & World Report envisions an America with a literacy rate of only 30%.

Before that America comes to be, you can stop it... by joining the fight against illiteracy today.

Call the Coalition for Literacy at toll-free **1-800-228-8813** and volunteer.

Volunteer Against Illiteracy. The only degree you need is a degree of caring.

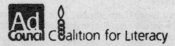

Ad Council Coalition for Literacy

Warner Books is proud to be an active supporter of the Coalition for Literacy.